# A REBEL'S PROMISE

## A SWEET SECOND CHANCE ADVENTURE ROMANCE

### SARA BLACKARD

*In memory of our retired sled dog, Mr. Butters.*
*Thanks for letting us race with you those last miles of your*
*journey.*

# 1

Gunnar Rebel crested the ridge overlooking the Mosquito Fork outside of Chicken, Alaska and called his sled dogs to a halt. The late February wind whipped against his face, sending a shiver down his spine even though he wore his thick parka. Smoke curled from the chimney of his grandparents' two-bedroom cabin his mom had grown up in. Rocky, Gunnar's lead dog, yipped and looked back at Gunnar like he'd lost his marbles stopping so close to home.

Gunnar shook his head and snorted. "Maybe I *have* lost my mind. Ever consider that?"

Rocky whined and cocked his head.

"Yeah? Not completely gone?" Gunnar rolled his shoulders. "You're probably right, but since I'm having a conversation with a dog that can't respond, I'm not sure I believe you." The fact that he said more words to his dogs than any human, even when he lived in civilization and not the end of the world, didn't escape his attention. "Come on, Rocky. Take us home."

Rocky yipped excitedly, prompting the other dogs to bark like a wild pack of wolves and lurch at their traces. Gunnar let the brake free and rocketed along the ridge. He still couldn't believe that he'd let Sunny, his baby sister, talk him into giving up his chance at racing the Yukon Quest and Iditarod that year in exchange for training for an expedition to the North Pole he might not even go on.

When she'd come to him with the news that Mason Steele, the owner of Nordic Canine Kibbles and an extreme adventurer, wanted to sponsor Gunnar, the news had shocked him. After spending the last fifteen years as an Air Force pararescueman, finding a sponsor his first year mushing shouldn't have happened, especially one as big as NCK. Having said sponsor stipulate that the support only came if Gunnar took the year off from racing and trained for a long-distance expedition to the North Pole had gotten an eyebrow raise, especially since he and Sunny were the replacements for if someone got injured on the actual team going to the Pole.

Being a PJ, he was used to adjusting mid-mission. In fact, his role as a pararescueman had prepared him to be an alternate, the back-up plan when things went wrong. That was their purpose in the military, rescue the special forces when missions went sideways. He'd just never been paid thousands to do it.

Not that he was complaining.

He leaned into the corner as Rocky led the dogs around the last bend home at a break-neck speed. He must want his warm bed and fish and kibble soup bad. Gunnar laughed at Rocky's smile and the way his tongue hung from his mouth. The dog loved it out here.

Gunnar did, too, though the solitude with no one but his dogs, Sunny, and her dogs as company may have fed into his anxiety around others, left over from his capture in the Afghanistan desert. He would probably adjust to life out of the military better if he'd stayed in Seward with Bjørn instead of jumping on the chance to escape into isolation. Not that he could pass up this opportunity. Too much money this year and in the future rode on him training for an expedition he wouldn't be going on.

However, he'd created the isolation by not going into Tok when Sunny did. He'd only ventured out of the quiet of the old cabin twice since Mason had offered the position. If Gunnar had missed Thanksgiving and Christmas at his parents' place south of Tok, his mama would've flown in to the homestead herself and tossed him onto the plane, hogtied if need be.

Knowing solitude only fed into his issues was one thing, taking the action needed to fix that was completely different. He'd use this winter to recoup, then get back to civilization and his dog sledding trips across the Resurrection Bay glaciers for tourists come spring. Maybe then participating in society wouldn't be like pulling teeth.

Gunnar let out a sigh as he pulled into the yard. The front door opened, and Sunny yanked on her parka as she stepped out of the cabin. She smiled and waved before rushing to help get the dogs off the line and to their kennels.

"Nice ride?" she asked over the barking of her own team's excitement at the dogs' return.

"Brisk, but not like December." Gunnar stripped off his heavy mittens and worked the first wheel dog off of the line.

She nodded. The three weeks of negative fifties and sixties had been brutal, but they'd trained through it. They were staying the winter in Chicken because of the extreme cold found there. Couldn't get that in Seward where the ocean kept the temperature hovering at a pleasant thirty above most of the winter.

After working in silence to get the dogs settled in their kennels, Gunnar stomped on the entryway and stepped into the cabin. The heat blasted from the wood stove, instantly causing him to sweat. He shucked his heavy parka and hung it by the door before heading to the kitchen to make the dogs their dinner.

"Just two more weeks and we can go back to the real world." Sunny closed the door with a sigh and hung her coat next to his.

"Yep." He didn't want to think of that fact.

"I know I said I needed to get away from people and their duplicity, but I think I've had enough of Chicken for a while." She pointed toward the old cookstove that doubled as their heat with her chin. "Need help?"

"Nah." He scooped the dry dog food out of the tote and filled the large stockpot of boiling fish heads and rice the rest of the way to the top.

"I'm not sure how Mama and Dad survived growing up here without going insane. I may not trust people right now, but I still like being around them, at least sometimes." Sunny plopped down on the threadbare couch that had been there since the seventies.

"Hmm." Gunnar didn't know what to say to that.

Since Sunny's business partner and friend had stolen all the money from their Denali guiding business and disappeared, leaving her with nothing, she'd become a shell of her normal, outgoing self. Normally, she lived up to her name in annoying abundance. Since everything was stolen from her last fall, she'd also lost that.

He'd wanted to call in some favors and find the jerk, but she'd made him swear he wouldn't. According to her, it was her own fault for being so gullible. A lesson she'd had to learn to find her actual path in life, whatever that meant.

"I guess they would've had each other and the other families living around here during that time. Crazy to think there used to be an actual community here year-round." Sunny picked up whatever romance she was reading today and flipped open the cover.

Gunnar had read more romances over the past months than he had any other genre. He should've thought that through and brought more than the measly handful of books he'd packed. He'd never admit to anyone, and had Sunny promise she'd not tell a soul, that he actually enjoyed the books she kept getting every week on the mail plane. She called them clean romance. Gunnar called them enlightening. Maybe if he ever got comfortable being close to others, he could put the knowledge found inked on the pages to use.

"Gonna feed the dogs." Gunnar lifted the pot with a grunt and headed toward the door.

Sunny jumped up from the table and rushed to open the door, only to pause with her hand on the handle. Gunnar shifted his boots, impatient to feed the dogs and get out of the rest of his gear.

"Do you hear that?" Sunny tipped her head to the side, a smile blooming across her face. "It's a plane."

"Yep." Gunnar motioned with the pot to the door.

"Sounds like Tiikâan's."

Sunny yanked open the door and pushed Gunnar out of the way. He chuckled low as she hopped from one foot to the next, struggling to get her snow boots on. As he headed to the dog yard, Tiikâan's bright, bumblebee yellow Piper PA-18 swooped over the cabin. Gunnar lifted the pot in greeting as the plane's wings tipped from side to side.

Gunnar continued to the dogs. They'd worked hard and deserved their dinner. Besides, his brother had to circle and check the landing area behind the cabin. Sunny and Gunnar kept it cleared and ready for planes, but an expert pilot always surveyed the runway before they touched down.

Giving each dog encouragement as he slopped their food in the bowls, Gunnar's eagerness to see his brother gave him hope. Hope that the time away had provided him a new perspective on life. He even hoped Tiikâan planned on staying a few days.

Gunnar set the empty pot on the porch and headed to the airstrip. Sunny danced in place, her hands clasped together in excitement. The Super Cub bounced on the snow-covered ground and quickly came to a stop ten feet from where he waited with Sunny. It still amazed him how his brother could land his plane in such a small area.

Sunny ran up to the door, and Gunnar ambled after her. He shoved his hands in his snow pants pockets as a shiver shook his body. He should've thrown on his parka before coming out here.

"Teee-khaan!" Sunny drew out their brother's name as she yelled in excitement, though he probably didn't hear her over the engine powering down.

Tiikâan pushed opened the door, a scowl on his face. Gunnar's stomach clenched. Had something happened and that's why Tiikâan was out there?

"Do you guys ever turn on your radio or fire up the computer?" He shook his head, motioning his arms to the wilderness surrounding them. "We've been trying to get a hold of you all day."

"What happened?" Gunnar crossed his arms, his focus tunneling to his brother.

"You're a go for the expedition, that's what happened." Tiikâan's face split with a smile, and the worry building in Gunnar's chest deflated in a whoosh.

"We're going?" Sunny gasped, her gaze darting between the two brothers. "Why?"

"Two of the people going were in an accident." Tiikâan shrugged, then quickly continued when Sunny covered her mouth in shock. "They're fine, but they won't be well enough to leave on time."

"We're going." Sunny dropped her hands, her eyes widening, followed by the first bright smile Gunnar had seen on her face since autumn. "We're going."

She whooped and threw her arms around Gunnar. He picked her up and spun in a circle. Her excitement infused Gunnar with adrenaline, making his heart race. He never imagined they'd actually get to go on the adventure of a lifetime. He'd been content just riding out the winter in Chicken. Now, though, trekking across the frozen Arctic Ocean would not only push his body to its limits, but force him to work with a team again.

Was he ready? He wasn't sure. Only knowing Sunny on the team put a lot of concern on him. Yet, maybe being in a life and death situation with others was what he needed to break through to his new life outside of the military.

A frigid wind rushed across the frozen pond, slicing into Julie Sparks's hood and skittering down her neck. It howled past her again with more force. Bare birch branches rattled like dry bones against each other as if in warning, then fell silent. She shivered and stomped her feet in the snow as her gaze darted through the forest.

"Come on, Jules." Her whisper sounded loud with the wind gone. "If you're freaking out in the outskirts of Fairbanks, how are you going to handle the expedition?"

If the expedition even happened now. With the Reeves's accident that afternoon, she wasn't sure venturing to the North Pole was possible. Mason Steele, their fearless leader, swore he had a plan, but he hadn't had the time to divulge it. When she realized she wasn't going to get any info, she'd come back to the bed-and-breakfast to get some sleep before the meeting in the morning.

Tolstoy, her lead dog and constant companion, leaned

against her leg and whined. He must think she's crazy, talking to herself. She rubbed his head to reassure him, though she wasn't sure herself.

She'd been on countless dogsled races through the Alaskan wilderness, had solo trained for years on week-long trips, had run both the Yukon Quest and Iditarod the previous year, finishing higher than any other rookie, and had never had nerves raging in her gut like a wolverine caught in a snare like she did now. She had tried working with her dogs. They'd sensed her unease, whining and pawing at her, so she'd left. She couldn't afford for them to be off their game.

Hanging out with the other guests lodging at the inn out toward Chena had only increased the suffocating sensation threatening to overwhelm her. She needed air. Needed space and the outdoors to calm her racing thoughts.

Her focus had to be on the next few days when the team finished any last-minute preparations before loading everything up and heading to Utqiagvik, formerly known as Barrow, Alaska. The frozen ocean between the expedition's launching point and the North Pole wouldn't go easy on her. She knew that from experience. The memory of her father being hauled into the rescue helicopter during his last dogsled race flitted to the front of her thoughts, but she quickly pushed it away.

She would not end up like her dad, dying of a heart attack on the trail like he always said he would. Not that she had anyone waiting at home for her. Her cousin, Saylor, didn't count, though she'd be devastated if anything happened to Julie.

Her lonely existence grated. She had no one to blame

but herself. Seemed easier after every romantic relationship petered out to nothing. It didn't really surprise her now. Her high school sweetheart, Gunnar Rebel, had taken her heart with him when he'd left her for the military, not once, but twice.

He hadn't even cared enough to respond to the letters she'd sent him after they'd reconnected that weekend seven years ago. She wasn't sure why she'd expected him to. Their agreement to sever ties so he could focus on being an Air Force Pararescueman hadn't changed. If anything, Gunnar had been more insistent about not contacting each other.

Of course, that decision had been before she'd gotten sick and needed his support.

But it hadn't come.

She'd learned she had enough strength of her own to survive. Survive being the key term, because for so long that had been the extent of her existence. Now, though, she'd found a sense of living she'd lost in the years after her illness. And that sense tangled completely in keeping her father's legacy alive. Well, not just keeping it alive, but elevating it to new heights.

She had to.

She had to make her life count, to do the incredible, for all those whose lives were cut short.

She'd push to her breaking point if need be, and the expedition from Alaska's northern shore to the North Pole could do it. Mason Steele's desire to do the impossible would be her proving ground. If she failed to get him to the Pole, his sponsorship and her future would crack and tumble into frigid oblivion. Oh, he hadn't come right out and said it, but the implication was there.

She wrapped her arms around her stomach as her meager dinner threatened to spew. The wind slapped her in the face, and she breathed the frigid freshness in. She squared her shoulders and turned to head back to the bed-and-breakfast.

Tolstoy trotted ahead of her, burying his head in the snow. She wished she could infuse his carefree manner into her bones. A wolf howled in the distance as a shiver raced through her. She stopped short on the edge of the yard, her heart pounding in her throat.

Doubts crept in from the thick darkness. Was she strong enough for such an intense expedition? Could she help lead them to their destination? What if she got off course and killed them all? She couldn't disappoint the memory of her father, couldn't let him down.

Her phone rang in her pocket, jolting her from her pathetic brooding. She rolled her eyes at her cousin Saylor's picture staring up at her from the screen. What could she possibly want now? Did she have some kind of ESP that told her Julie was in complete freak-out mode?

She cleared her throat, hoping her pity party didn't linger in her voice. "Hello?"

"Hey. I just heard about the accident. What's going to happen now?" Saylor's clipped tone pulled Julie back from her fretting even more.

"I don't know. Mason says he has a plan. He's laying it all out tomorrow morning at ten." Julie stared at the lights shining from the bed-and-breakfast's windows.

"I have a meeting with a supplier for Ascent at nine-thirty I can't miss." Saylor's tapping on her computer came over the phone.

Julie didn't know how her cousin could handle everything she did. Not only was she the head of distribution for the outdoor supply company, Ascent, Inc., but Mason had talked her into overseeing the expedition's base. She'd be the one coordinating the resupply stops along the trail, which made sense given the large chunk of change Ascent contributed to the expedition. It was a massive undertaking, but if anyone could do it, Saylor could. She always excelled at being in charge.

"I'll let Mason know you'll be late." Julie threaded her fingers through Tolstoy's fur as he sat next to her with a whine.

"I could strangle that man right now for his lack of info. Would it kill him to send out a quick text to fill us in?" Saylor growled.

She tended to be intense. It made her a little scary sometimes, but Julie loved that about her cousin. They were the exact opposites, which Julie had needed when things got rough.

A shiver raked through Julie. "You know Mason. He probably figures there's no need to discuss it until we're together."

"Yeah. He's got efficiency going for him," Saylor grumbled.

She couldn't fault him for that, not with how focused she was. Julie smiled at her cousin's exasperation, then sobered. Until they knew what was going on, Julie would be in a knot of nerves.

"Listen, I'm going to turn in. I'll see you tomorrow." Patting Tolstoy on the head, she headed into the bed-and-breakfast, glad the owners were friends and let her keep her lead dog with her.

"Yep. Love you," Saylor said.

"Love you too." Julie would thank God every day for Saylor.

Walking in the back door of the inn, she stripped her mittens off in the sudden heat and tucked them into her pockets. If Mason's back-up plan worked, the next few days would be full of preparations that she needed to focus on. She couldn't afford to be distracted by her doubts and fears.

She shrugged out of her coat and hung it on an empty hook, exhaustion from her emotions making her arms feel like lead. She needed sleep and maybe a good amount of prayer if she expected to make it to launch day.

"Come on, Tolstoy." She scratched behind her friend's ear. "Let's go turn in."

Turning the corner to the bedrooms, she ran into a solid body with a grunt. Her hands splayed across a well-muscled chest as she tried to keep from falling over. How could her skin tingle under her layers of sweater and shirts where strong hands kept her upright?

"Sorry." Her face heated at her clumsiness, and she tucked her head.

Could she escape to her room without making a complete fool of herself?

"Jules?" The hands tightened around her waist, stopping her retreat.

The voice she hadn't heard for seven years, but that had tortured her in her dreams, whipped her head up. Dark, almost black eyes stared at her in shock. So, Gunnar Rebel was back in Alaska. Could his timing be any worse?

## 3

---

Gunnar's fingers flexed against Julie's waist, his skin tingling against the contact. She had changed little since the last time he'd seen her. The years apart had only made her more beautiful. Her light brown hair hung long down her back. Red rimmed her hazel eyes like she'd been crying, just like they'd been the day he'd left. His heart clenched and his brow furrowed.

Could he fix what had made her sad?

Swallowing, he dropped his hands like the contact had burned him. He couldn't help her. He'd killed that chance seven years before when he'd foolishly crushed their love and friendship with his selfishness a second time.

"Gunnar." Julie's voice shook as she took a step back.

He shoved his hands in his jeans pockets. Her hand trembled as it rubbed her cheek. He hated that he made her nervous, but his heart flipped at her bare ring finger.

Not that it meant anything. Lots of women didn't wear wedding rings.

"You okay?" He inwardly cringed at the loaded question that she could take any number of ways.

"Yeah. You just startled me, is all." She glanced down at the dog next to her, then lifted her face to him. "So, you on leave?"

"No."

"Oh. You're out of the Air Force then?" Her words held a hesitancy that tore at his heart.

"Yep." *Speak, dummy! String two, preferably more, words together.* "I retired last year."

"That's ... great."

She didn't sound thrilled. In fact, if he was a betting man, she wasn't excited about seeing him at all. He'd secretly hoped if they ever saw each other, they could patch things up, but, like so many other things his decisions had destroyed, it was obvious their relationship was one of them.

Loneliness like he'd never felt before hit him in the gut like a well-placed jab.

"You here for the Quest?" See, he could hold a conversation.

"Nope." She pulled her bottom lip between her teeth. "Well, I'm exhausted. It was good seeing you."

The platitude rang hollow, as fake as her forced smile.

"Yeah." He wanted to say more.

Wanted to tell her he'd missed her every single day since he left.

To beg her to forgive him for ruining their friendship.

Before he could drum up the courage, she stepped around him. Her soft footsteps faded down the hall. He should go after her. He turned to watch her leave. Maybe he could convince her to have breakfast with him? Catch up for old time's sake. She couldn't hate him so much that she wouldn't do that, could she?

The memory of the two unopened letters she'd sent to him forced its way to the surface of Gunnar's scrambling thoughts. They burned a hole in his conscience, just like they had burned to be pulled out and opened from where he'd kept them in his pack for the last seven years.

She opened her door and disappeared inside, never once glancing back at him. The quiet click of the door shutting caused Gunnar to flinch. He hung his head, tears stinging his eyes. He didn't deserve a minute of her time, not after what he'd done. It was better to just let things go. It was what he'd done all those years ago. He couldn't expect to change that decision now.

## 4

Early the next morning, Julie banged on the cabin door her cousin Saylor had rented for the week, praying she wouldn't ask too many questions. Shifting from one foot to the other, Julie glanced back to her cousin's truck parked in the driveway. She was definitely here.

The deadbolt clicked, and Julie whipped her head back to the door. "What took you so long?"

"Wow. Good morning to you too." Saylor's wet hair dripped onto her bare shoulders. A large towel wrapped around her. "You okay?"

No, Julie wasn't okay, but she couldn't let her cousin know why. Saylor stepped back and motioned Julie in.

"I'm fine." She forced a smile when Saylor's eyebrow rose.

"You sure? Because the way you were banging down the door, I thought for sure someone had died or something." Saylor closed the door and shivered.

"No, nothing like that." Julie sighed and turned to her cousin. "Can I stay with you? I can sleep on the floor."

"Yeah, sure. I'd love to have you here before you leave." Saylor hiked the towel higher. "What's wrong with the B&B?"

"Nothing. It's great, just … crowded." Julie rushed on before Saylor could point out Julie usually enjoyed being around people. "There are a lot of other mushers there getting ready for the Quest." Not a lie. "I just need to be somewhere that doesn't have a million dogs barking and people sizing each other up."

Not so true. She loved the atmosphere that bubbled the few days before the Yukon Quest started. She'd spent every February in that sphere for as long as she could remember. Part of the inn's appeal was how they hosted Quest runners each year, but there was no way she could be in the same house as Gunnar. She thought she could. All night long she had tried to talk herself into believing it wouldn't be a big deal, but she couldn't.

Not now.

Maybe next year when she could mentally prepare herself.

She shook her head.

Probably not.

He'd just gotten more handsome with his rugged beard and piercing dark eyes. He'd built himself some nice muscles under that shirt she'd had the misfortune of pressing her hands against. She didn't think she could ever prepare herself for being around all that. Plus, the awkwardness between them depressed her, tore at her heart that was already nothing but tatters. Kind of sucked to find out after all these years, she still had enough heart left to pound at the sight of him.

Exactly why she had to leave. She couldn't let his sudden return distract her from getting ready for the expedition. One mistake could cost the team their safety and reaching the Pole. There was no way she'd let herself be the weak link, not after how hard she'd worked to prove she belonged.

Saylor's eyes narrowed at Julie, making her break out in a sweat. "What's going on with you? You're acting weird."

"Nothing's going on with me." Why'd Julie's voice get all squeaky?

"You know I can read you like a book, right? And not the classic literature kind. You're a picture book to me." Saylor circled her finger at Julie's face. "There is so much happening on your pretty little face right now. In fact, your entire body is one of those fancy pop-up books, all this excitement in 3D."

Saylor crossed her arms over her chest, making Julie swallow. She had to come up with something, but her brain was half scrambled like a pan full of runny eggs. Her gaze darted around the little room.

"I'm just nervous about the expedition, is all. I don't want the distraction of others right now." She tucked a loose hair behind her ear.

Her hasty braid had come apart in her rush to leave the inn. Letting out a slow breath, she stared Saylor down. Saylor held her gaze for so long, Julie worried she'd break.

"Okay." Saylor shrugged and stepped toward the

bathroom. "There's only one bed, but it's a king so we won't have to cuddle."

"Oh, I'll just camp out on the floor. I'm okay with that." Julie let her gaze wander the cute cabin, willing her tight muscles to relax.

"Jules, what part of 'king bed' didn't you understand? There's plenty of room for both of us plus half your dog team, and I'm not letting your last few nights of warmth and comfort be spent sleeping on the floor." Saylor shook her head, calling over her shoulder as she entered the bathroom.

She snapped the door shut with a chuckle. Julie slumped onto the couch and plopped her head in her hands. She hated she was so twisted up over her run-in with Gunnar. Maybe she should've stayed and faced the giant, so to speak. Then she wouldn't have this sense that she had scurried into hiding.

Which was exactly what she did.

"Ugh, why'd he have to show up now? Why not after the expedition? Or here's a thought, why'd he have to show up at all?" She pushed her hands through her hair, yanking even more hair from her braid. "And why'd I have to be thrown off balance?"

"By who?" Saylor's question startled a yelp out of Julie.

"No one." Her quick retort wasn't convincing, even to herself.

"I knew something was up." Saylor stepped over Julie's legs and sank into the couch, making Julie fall into her.

Julie gave into the motion and leaned her head on Saylor's shoulder. "It's nothing."

"Oh, no." Saylor pushed Julie off her shoulder. "You don't get off that easy."

"Seriously, I just want to focus on the expedition. Nothing else matters."

"Jules, you never get flustered. Ever. So, whoever has you in a tizzy did a bang-up job of it." Saylor's eyes narrowed. "Do I have to go over there and take care of things? I know you're a softy, so I'll do it if I have to."

As the office manager at Ascent, Inc., the leading distributor and manufacturer of outdoor gear, Saylor could put the fear of God into people. Julie had seen it when she stayed a couple of weeks with Saylor. A supplier hadn't followed through on their delivery, and Saylor's icy calm had made Julie want to jump to attention. Her employees loved her, though. Would practically climb mountains for her, which was good since the company's primary focus was climbing gear.

"No, you can't go over there." Julie shook her head. The image of Saylor standing toe to toe with Gunnar was horrifying.

"Hey, just tell me. You're worrying me, and I have enough of that with running all the base communications and resupply checkpoints for the expedition." Saylor slid her hand into Julie's and gave a quick squeeze.

Julie closed her gritty, sleep-deprived eyes and leaned back on the couch cushions. "Gunnar was there. I ran into him. Literally crashed right into his solid chest."

She flexed her free hand, the tingle still there from the contact with him.

"Why that—" Saylor moved to get up, but Julie held tight to her hand. "I've been waiting years to give that piece of owl puke my thoughts."

"No, Saylor, it's fine." Julie wrapped her free hand around Saylor's arm and pulled her cousin back against her side. "I didn't really talk to him. Basically beelined for my room and locked myself in for the rest of the night."

"Why'd you do that? After what he did to you, you should've blasted him. Singed him until all that was left of him was burned bones."

"Saylor, he did nothing to me but keep his promise. I never expected him to come running back." Julie was full of lies that morning. "We'd promised not to contact each other. I broke that promise. If anything, he should singe me."

"What about the promise you two made to always be there for each other? Remember that one? I do. You gushed on and on about it during the summer when I came to stay with you after our freshman year of high school. You two made that promise first. It supersedes any promises made after."

"I always knew he would go into the military. It's almost all he talked about, even before we started dating and were just friends. His promise to himself and to the soldiers he swore he'd protect surpasses everything else. I'd just had a moment of weakness and forgot."

Saylor stood with a huff, ripping her arm out of Julie's grip.

"A moment of weakness?" Her shrill voice filled the cabin as she paced to the kitchen and turned, her face splotched red with anger. "Seriously? Finding out you have cancer and almost dying isn't a moment of weakness. It's a deep hole of despair. When you needed him, he went back on his word to you. Yes, his service to the country was commendable, but his disregard to you, your friendship, and your love is the most dishonorable action I've ever seen." She crossed her arms over her chest and stared at the bathroom.

Her words stabbed at Julie's heart, condensing the hurt she had felt at Gunnar's silence into dull bitterness. Saylor was right, but so was Julie. She never should've sent those letters in the first place.

"You know what? I'm glad he's there. I'm going to go give that sorry sack of moose nuggets a piece of my mind." Saylor stomped to the door, and Julie vaulted over the coffee table.

"No. Just leave it be." Julie slammed her hand against the door and angled her body between it and her cousin.

"Jules, he can't get away with treating you like he did."

"It was seven years ago. I'm over it, over him. Dragging it all up to the surface won't do any good now." Julie pushed on Saylor's shoulder.

"Julie—"

"Please, I'd rather just forget it all, forget him. I had. It's just seeing him for the first time in so long just kind of threw me off-kilter, but I'm good."

Saylor stared Julie down, her cheek clenching as she searched deep into Julie's soul. She had let the past go years before. She just hoped Saylor didn't see the hurt and love still embedded within.

"Fine. I won't go rip his head from his shoulders." Saylor held her hands up in surrender and backed away from the door.

Julie sagged against the wood. "Besides, Alaska's a big state. It's not like I'll be seeing him soon, if ever again."

Those words should be a relief. Somehow, to her horror, they weren't.

## 5

G unnar surveyed the eating area again. Not that anything had changed. Or, more to the point, that Julie hadn't arrived as he sat at the corner table for over an hour. He'd never ate egg casserole and pancakes so slowly. Now, he was nursing his eighth cup of coffee, trying not to be obvious that he was waiting for a brown-headed bombshell to saunter in for breakfast.

Bomb described her perfectly. A compact grenade that blew up right in front of his face, exploding his entire world into chaos. He hadn't slept. Had lain awake all night, his mind unwilling to let go of the fact that she was under the same roof as him for the first time in seven years. All the memories he'd lived off of during the quiet moments of waiting for action, all the small moments with her he'd focused on to get through the interrogations and torture of his capture by the enemy, barreled through his mind over and over the entire night.

He had to see her again, to talk to her with more than just one syllable grunts. He should be used to waiting.

Inactivity had totaled more days than action in his service to the country. Yet, sitting in the dining room, counting each second for her arrival, whittled his patience down with each click of the clock hand.

Standing with a jerk, he piled his dirty dishes, took them to the sink, and stalked out of the room. He couldn't sit there anymore. He'd just knock on her door and ask if she wanted to join him for breakfast. Though the copious amount of coffee and food he'd already consumed practically pushed up his esophagus, he'd eat again if it meant he could visit with her.

He stopped outside her door and raised his hand to knock.

What was he doing?

She wouldn't want to join him for coffee, not after what he'd done. That much was obvious with how quickly she had beat a retreat the night before. He lowered his hand and hung his head, guilt and pain settling across his shoulders, weighing him down.

Seeing her again had been like a shot of sunshine straight into his veins. Having her in front of him, getting a whiff of her strawberry shampoo, made him realize how all his memories were just a faded version of her. While they'd helped him stay sane in difficult times, they didn't do her justice, not really.

He needed to see her again, even if it was to brighten his memories to sustain him for the stretch of years before him. Straightening his shoulders back, he lifted his hand and rapped two sharp knocks on the wood.

"You're not gonna find Julie there." The innkeeper's voice from farther down the hall startled Gunnar.

He dropped his fist to hide the discomfort of someone

sneaking up on him, shoving his hand into his pocket. "No?"

"Nope." The older man with a thick beard and friendly eyes shifted the stack of sheets in his arms. "She checked out this morning."

"Oh." Disappointment sliced through him so sharply he looked down at his chest to see if he bled. "Thanks."

"Sorry, son." The man continued past Gunnar while he stared at the floor.

Had she left because of him? Gunnar snorted, hurt building in his chest. Of course, she left because of him. He'd been a horrible friend, throwing Julie's trust into the raging Tanana River by not opening her letters, even if she broke their promise not to contact each other.

He didn't deserve breakfast with her. Didn't deserve the brief interaction he got the night before. A slap across the face? That would be justified. Punch in the gut? He deserved even more.

He'd been foolish to expect she'd join him over coffee.

Foolish and selfish.

"Hey! You eat yet?" Sunny rounded the corner, heading toward the dining area.

"Yeah." He turned to her, not missing the way her gaze darted to Julie's door and back with a lift of her eyebrow.

He crossed his arms. No way was he telling his sister. Sunny had only been eight when he'd left for basic, but she'd idolized Julie. Sunny's constant shadowing any time Julie had come over to hang out had been both frustrating as her boyfriend and one reason he had loved her so much. She'd fit in, dishing out encouragement and honest affection to his family just as easily as she did to him. His leaving and her finding out Julie wouldn't be coming around anymore had devastated Sunny.

"All righty then. I'm going to grab something to go, then we can head into town for the meeting." Sunny stomped past, muttering under her breath about annoying, taciturn brothers.

Gunnar smirked, then stilled the motion. It was better that Julie had gone. He didn't need the distraction. Didn't need his attention pulled from preparing for the expedition. Lots of work had to be done in the next few days to get caught up with the rest of the team. Not having the temptation to run back to the inn to catch a glimpse of Julie was for the best. Besides, dragging up the past brought nothing but hurt to the surface.

## 6

J ulie stomped down the hall to the meeting room. Mason had rented the small building at the airstrip so they could load the planes that would take them to Barrow directly from the hangar instead of having to transport everything. The smart move meant she could really spread the supplies out and check everything closely.

The entire drive to the hangar had worry knotting in her stomach. Mason would figure out how to make the expedition a go. His calm, steady demeanor had been the main reason she'd agreed to go on the expedition. Well, that and the fact if she didn't, she'd probably lose his sponsorship.

The expedition had started out as something she had to do for her kennel and her father's legacy. Training with the team the last four months had transformed the trip into something she looked forward to, even despite her momentary breakdown the night before. Her team would attempt the incredible. How could she not be excited?

She stepped into the room only to find Mason and his best friend—expedition physician, Clark Simms—bent over the computer at the table. Mason and Clark had many adventures under their belt together, from scaling Denali to mushing across Antarctica. They'd crossed the Sahara by camel and kayaked the Amazon River. If there was an adventure to conquer, these two men were bound to do it. She couldn't let the stress of preparing make her forget how blessed she was to be a part of their next conquest.

"Morning, boys." Since the two of them liked to joke and mess around like children, she'd started calling them boys.

Normally, they smiled at the term with a twinkle of mischief in their eyes. At the moment, their matching frowns pulled her own mouth down.

"How are the Reeves?" She took a deep breath, darting her eyes from one man to the next.

The Reeves were a couple from Eagle that took guests on adventures through the northern wilderness. Both being paramedics and having extensive mushing backgrounds made them invaluable members on the team. Over the last four months, Julie depended on their steady assurance.

"They're fine." Clark rounded the table and draped his arm across her shoulder, leading her to a chair. "Just injured. Mary has a concussion and dislocated shoulder, and Jack's femur snapped in half. Thankfully, they weren't hurt worse, though their truck is totaled."

"Thank God." She slumped into the seat with a huff.

"Glad I had a back-up plan." Mason's words snapped

her head up. He shrugged. "I always have a back-up plan."

"Okay. How are we going to get to the North Pole with two fewer people on the team?" Julie crossed her arms over her chest, still a little cross at him for not clueing them all in yesterday.

"I had fill-ins training just in case something like this happened."

Smart, except it was like adding a new forward and goalie to the team just as you headed into the Stanley Cup.

"I don't know. We've melded as a solid unit these last four months. We know each other so well we can communicate without a word. Isn't it dangerous to throw two new people into the mix we don't even know?" She hated pointing that out when Mason had everything planned, but one wrong move on the Arctic Ocean could mean death.

"I have total confidence that these two will fit in just fine." Mason's gaze went to the door and relief softened the creases at the corner of his eyes. "Good. Just in time."

Julie turned in her seat as Gunnar Rebel stepped into the room behind a woman who had to be one of his sisters. Was she little Sunny? It was a good thing Julie's behind was already parked in a seat, otherwise she would've been on the floor. Her entire body trembled.

Gunnar's gaze connected with hers, his eyebrows shooting to his hairline in shock. Good. At least she wasn't the only one in the dark. She couldn't do this, could she? Couldn't spend the next unknown number of days and nights trekking over the frozen ocean with the man who hadn't been there when she'd needed it most.

She should say something, anything, to get Mason to make a different decision. She turned to him, her mind spinning with options that didn't include Gunnar Rebel.

Mason extended his arm to the door. "This is—"

"Jules?" Sunny interrupted Mason. "Julie Sparks?"

Julie turned back to the door and lifted her hand in a pitiful wave. "Sunny?"

Sunny peeked back at her brother, worry crinkling her forehead, before she smoothed it out and closed the distance between them. "It's so good to see you."

Julie stood and stiffly returned Sunny's hug. "You too."

"You all know each other?" Mason asked.

"We used to hang out all the time before Gunnar enlisted." Sunny answered Mason, then focused back on Julie.

Julie prayed Sunny wouldn't give Mason and Clark all the details about their connected past.

"Good. Then this transition should be easier than I thought." Mason sat in the chair and motioned to the others to do the same. "Sit. We have a lot to discuss."

Julie felt Gunnar's eyes on her. Felt the heat of his gaze swirl to settle uncomfortably in her gut. She ignored him, staring at the seat in front of her like it was an electric chair, and she was going to her execution.

She should say something, ask Mason to talk privately. Heck, she could channel Saylor and demand someone else. Anyone else.

"Julie?" Mason lifted an eyebrow.

She swallowed and wiped her slick hands on her jeans as she slid into the chair. She couldn't make a scene, not with everyone here. The conversation buzzed in her ears as she spent the next hour figuring out how to convince Mason that taking the Rebels wasn't a good idea. Because one thing was for sure, she couldn't spend countless nights in a tiny tent with the man who'd broken her heart. The man her foolish heart still trembled for.

## 7

Gunnar walked to the hangar the team used to organize their supplies. Julie had excused herself over an hour ago, stating that she had work to do. He didn't doubt it. Preparing for an expedition like theirs took paying attention to every little detail. He also didn't doubt that her escape from the office had just as much to do with him as the work she had.

Maybe more.

He sighed and peeked through the tall, skinny window in the door. He hadn't missed the way she didn't look at him once after the initial shock. Her soft, distracted answers had screamed her wheels were turning, probably figuring out a way to get him kicked off the expedition.

She bent over a pallet of dog food, counting the bags, then checking her clipboard. Maybe he should do her a favor and stay behind? Surely there was someone else qualified to go.

He shoved his hands in his pockets as his eyes tracked

her to a pile of rope on a table. Her light brown braid fell over her shoulder as she picked up the tangled mess. The look on her face was one he'd seen many times in their relationship. It was the look she'd get when the dogs took off after a rabbit or tangled themselves on the line in their excitement to run. She also had given it when he had distracted her from a job.

In the past, he'd been able to smooth the frustrated expression with a soft touch or a well-placed kiss. That definitely wouldn't work now. Trying that would probably get him a fist to the face, though knowing Julie, she wouldn't do that even if he deserved it.

He closed his eyes with a sigh. There was no way he could pull out of the expedition. Mason had brought Gunnar onto the team because of his history as a PJ. No one could look at a situation and find a solution like he could. No one could keep Julie and the rest of them safe like him.

He opened his eyes, his attention instantly on her. Whether she liked it or not, he couldn't leave their safety to someone else. He'd go crazy with worry if he did.

"Well, here we go." He yanked the door open and strode through. Nothing like spending time with the love of his life who hated his guts to put some pep in his step. "How can I help?"

Julie flinched, dropping the rope, her hands shaking as she turned to him. Her pale skin and hunched shoulders made him feel like the biggest jerk in Alaska. Heck, the world.

She whipped her head back to the rope. "I've got things under control. Thanks, though."

"I don't mind. Nothing else to do." Gunnar surveyed

the orderly stacks of supplies and gear.

"Really, I—"

The main door to outside swung open, blasting the hangar with frigid air. It was the perfect distraction from the chilly conversation.

"Phew, it's cold. You sure you want to trek across the frozen ocean in this? Sane people stay inside where their boogers don't freeze instantly in their nose." Saylor Reed, Julie's cousin, hadn't changed a bit since he'd last seen her in high school. She stomped the snow off her feet and shook out her coat. "Seriously, it's like two-second snot freeze right now."

When she finally lifted her head, she froze, her eyes narrowing to slits. "You."

"Hey." Gunnar nodded at her, not knowing what to say.

"What are you doing here?" A brilliant shade of red bloomed up her neck. "Did you follow Julie?"

Gunnar didn't know what to say to that accusation. The silent pause hung like the fog on the mountains in the morning, cold and slicking the skin.

"Gunnar and his sister Sunny are replacing the Reeves on the expedition," Julie answered for him, her voice thick with resignation.

"No." Saylor shook her head. "Sunny is amazing, but this waste of air?" Saylor waved her hand at Gunnar.

"Saylor," Julie cautioned.

"You can't count on him." Saylor threw her arms out wide as the door behind him opened and Sunny's perfume filtered through the hangar smells to Gunnar.

Julie slammed the tangled rope on the table, making Gunnar and Saylor flinch. "Gunnar, you can help by unknotting this rope. I need to check on something." Her voice trembled at the end of her sentence, and she rushed to the door leading to the offices. "Come with me," she whispered to her cousin as she walked past.

Without waiting, Julie pushed past Gunnar and Sunny and disappeared down the hall. Gunnar stared after Julie, ignoring the heat of Saylor's presence as she stepped into his bubble. She poked him hard in the chest.

"Don't even think about it. After what you did to her, you don't even deserve to look at her." Her cheeks clenched, and tears of anger brightened her eyes. "Supposedly, you're all about honor and loyalty, more like selfish ambition, if you ask me. When she needed you, really needed you, you couldn't be bothered." Her voice cracked, sending a snake slithering down Gunnar's spine that left him feeling gritty. "You can't be trusted, not when it really counts, and I will not sit by and let you abandon her again."

She pushed past Gunnar, her words more than her force making him stumble a step back. Sunny's mouth flapped, and she reached for Saylor as she stormed by. The snake that had slithered down his spine, coiled in his gut.

His sister turned wide eyes to him. "What was that about?"

Gunnar swallowed the lump in his throat and shook his head.

Two letters stashed in his pack would probably enlighten him. Closing his eyes, he dropped his head as the snake rolled a nauseating flip and tried to slither up his throat. He just wasn't sure he was brave enough to open them.

## 8

J ulie rushed down the hall, not caring where she went as long as she got away. She'd vacillated over the last hour between believing she could push through the discomfort of being around Gunnar again to trying to convince Mason that there was a better option. Racking her brain for someone, anyone, who could take the Reeves's place besides Gunnar had left her with a headache. She had a solid list of qualified mushers and outdoor enthusiasts, but getting them here and ready to go in the next two days would be borderline impossible. Plus, from what Mason had said in the meeting, the Rebels had been training the entire winter from their place in Chicken.

Julie stopped and leaned against the wall. Her cheeks heated. The blush had nothing to do with the anger and embarrassment of the confrontation in the hangar and everything to do with the memory of her and Gunnar's last time spent at the old cabin in Chicken. Many of the overnight mushing trips in high school took them to that cabin. Nothing had ever happened beyond kissing. Until that last trip seven years ago when they'd run into each other while he was home on leave and had decided to go on a mushing trip for old time's sake to catch up.

"You have got to be kidding me." Saylor's angry words ripped Julie back from the past.

"Shh, you don't have to shout." Julie pushed off the wall and continued to the front door. Maybe if she left, got some fresh air and checked on her dogs, she'd come back with a calmer mind.

"Oh, I most certainly do."

That's her cousin, always taking charge.

"I can handle this, Saylor. You don't have to raise a fuss." Julie turned around and held up her hands for Saylor to calm down. The last thing Julie needed was for Saylor to make it worse. "You didn't have to be so rude back there, you know."

"Oh, he hasn't seen rude yet. I'm about to go napalm on this expedition." Saylor cracked her knuckles and glanced toward the office that Mason had parked his stuff in.

"Saylor, no. Just stay out of it, please." Julie grabbed her cousin's arm and pulled her away from the offices.

"I'm not about to let that caribou snot anywhere near you, let alone depend on him for your safety." Saylor was in rare form today.

Julie's eyes darted past her cousin to the offices, her heart pounding in her chest so hard her throat hurt. Julie hated confrontation. Hated disappointing others and causing problems. She didn't want to draw attention to herself, especially in such a pathetic way. She didn't want to come across as the scorned ex-girlfriend, so she had to get Saylor under control before she made this entire situation worse.

"Please, would you calm down? I can't think with you radiating anger and spewing hate." Julie rubbed Saylor's arm, willing her to let the negativity go.

Julie's battle with cancer had changed Saylor. Sure, she'd always been brash and assertive, but when Julie got sick, Saylor's need to challenge life kicked into overdrive. She also wasn't one to let an offense go, even if the affront wasn't directed at her. Gunnar not contacting Julie all those years ago was something Saylor saw as unforgivable, even though Julie explained over and over that his silence was what they'd agreed to.

Saylor said his silence was weakness, cowardice. She once told Julie she never wanted to be seen as weak, and no one would ever consider calling her that. Well, and expect to come away with all their fingers intact. Normally, Julie loved how passionate Saylor was about everything she put her mind to. Now, though, she wished her cousin would take on passivity for a moment so Julie could escape here without a scene.

"I'm going to talk to Mason—"

"Please, you'll back down the minute he looks at you." Saylor's comment, while true, pinched. "If he doesn't take Gunnar off the expedition, Ascent Inc. will pull their portion of the funding."

"Don't you dare." Julie yanked on Saylor's arm as she stepped toward the offices. "Don't even suggest such a thing. It's petty and would make Ascent look bad. You don't want that."

Saylor crossed her arms over her chest with a huff.

Julie dropped her voice. "It also makes me look like I

haven't moved past high school. That I'm not only pathetic, but weak. Don't ruin this for me."

"What's going on?" Mason stepped out of his office, his gray eyes darting between the two women.

"Nothing." Julie quickly forced the word out.

Saylor lifted her eyebrow and hissed a whisper. "Tell him or I will."

A tightness tingled in Julie's chest and rushed up her face, making her lightheaded. She didn't want to say anything, didn't want the conflict, but if she didn't, Saylor would go all Mount Vesuvius on them and bury them all in volcanic demands.

"Saylor, I need to run and grab some medical supplies that just got in. Care to join me?" Clark motioned toward the door, his head tipping to Mason.

Julie liked Clark. His easy manner and helpfulness was so opposite of Mason's enthusiastic rush through life. Mason came up with the adventure, and Clark helped him conquer it. At the moment, Julie considered him the bravest man alive, with his willingness to distract Saylor in her agitated state.

"Fine." Saylor adjusted her coat she hadn't taken off yet and stomped to the door. "But we're going to the Cookie Jar while we're out. I need carbs and sugar."

"I'd love to go out to lunch with you, Saylor. I haven't had a date in a long, long time." Clark snatched his coat from the rack as Saylor froze while opening the door.

"This isn't a date." She stared him down, but his lip just lifted on one side.

"If you say so." Was he really interested in Saylor or just diffusing the tension?

Saylor whipped out the door. With a wink at Julie,

Clark followed Saylor out. Nerves jostled in her, leaving her in a cold sweat. She stared at the door, building up her confidence, because she wasn't sure she could look at Mason and tell him what was wrong.

"All right, the little hurricane left. What do you need to talk to me about?" Mason's description of Saylor was spot on.

Taking a deep breath, Julie pulled her big girl panties up. She would tell him her concerns about Gunnar, then get on with getting prepared.

"It's about Gunnar." Her voice cracked. So much for showing confidence.

Mason's forehead creased. "There's a problem?"

"Yeah." Julie took another deep breath and forged ahead. "I've dealt with Gunnar in the past. I'm just ... I'm not sure I can be on the team with him. That I can trust him to be there when we need him."

There. She'd said it. It was the truth, so why did guilt coat her mouth like she'd eaten a handful of bitter pumpkin berries?

Mason glanced down the hall toward the hangar, his jaw clenching as he thought. The silence stretched on, and Julie shifted on her feet. She should say something, explain the situation or take the words back. Yet, her cowardice won out, gluing her mouth shut.

Mason sighed, rubbed his hand across the back of his neck, then turned his gaze on her. "I'm sorry to hear that. And I hate to say this, but if you don't think you can work with Gunnar, you'll have to stay behind."

She gaped at him, her veins flooding cold through her body. How could Mason pick Gunnar so quickly when she'd been working her tail off for the last four months?

"Julie, we need you on the team. We really do. You've been mushing for ages and your wilderness skills are amazing, plus you have a way about you that just calms the rest of us when we're agitated." Mason's words should make her proud, but it just made her lightheaded. "But Gunnar and Sunny have been training hard all winter in the off chance something like this happened. His experience in the military, both in medical trauma and emergency situations, is a necessity. If something happens to Clark, none of us can do what Gunnar can. With the Reeves gone, we'd only have one medical expert. That's a risk I just can't take."

He sighed, and she felt a stab into her chest. "I'm sorry, Julie, but if you can't work with Gunnar, then you can't go."

## 9

Gunnar trudged to his room at the bed-and-breakfast later that evening. His backpack, slung over his shoulder, grew heavier with each step. He'd stayed, gotten the rope untangled, helped pack boxes, and double-checked the medical supplies. He did everything Julie asked him to do after she came back into the hangar, though the letters screamed at him to rip them open and finally read them.

She'd been pale, her shoulders slumped. Neither of them spoke beyond a sentence here and there. Her reaction and Saylor's words left him nauseated, like at any moment he'd have to dash out the door and toss his cookies in the snowbank.

Not that he had any cookies to toss.

With the churn in his gut and the dread of reading the letters, he hadn't been able to eat since breakfast. After Saylor's blow up, he couldn't not read them.

Not anymore.

His legs felt like two thousand-pound musk oxen had

settled in them as he made his way to his room. He couldn't remember feeling this amount of exhaustion and pain that weighed on him, even on the worst day of training and when he'd been captured by terrorists and tortured. The Air Force had always told them that mental assaults could take more out of you than physical. His training, and later his capture, had taught him that firsthand.

Yet, none of that prepared him for having to slide his finger between two pieces of paper and read why Saylor said he can't be trusted. That he had abandoned Julie.

He ran a hand over his heart, trying to ease the ache there. Yeah, those words had hit their mark. He doubted the pain would get any better.

Easing the key into the handle, he pushed the door open with a leaden arm. Shutting it behind him, he snapped the lock with a click, then let the backpack slide from his shoulder. He looked down at it where it dangled from his fingers.

He didn't want to open it. Didn't want to pull the letters from the interior pocket they'd been in for the last seven years. How many times had he taken them out and just stared at them? How many times had Julie's curly handwriting gotten him through rough days? Had he fallen asleep with them pressed to his chest?

He never deserved to take the comfort they provided him, not when he hadn't had the decency to even open them. He'd allowed himself to think she'd written because she'd missed him. That she had hoped their unexpected rendezvous meant they could have a relationship again.

That she was proud of him.

Closing his eyes, his teeth clenched and spiked pain to his temple. He was selfish, just like Saylor said. He wished he could travel back in time and knock some sense into his young, cocky self. Since time travel wasn't possible, he could only move forward. Moving forward meant reading why Julie had really written to him when they'd promised not to.

He lurched toward the bed like he was going to his execution. His backpack dragged across the worn carpet. The bed squeaked when he sat on it, but he barely registered it. Just like he could hardly hear the boisterous talking in the main room above the ringing in his ears.

He took a deep breath and pulled the pack to his lap. Cutting his prayer for strength off, he unzipped the bag. He didn't deserve comfort or help right now, not after he'd waited so long.

The paper was soft and familiar against his fingertips as he eased them out of their hiding place. He set the pack to the side and flipped the envelopes over in his hands. Laying the second letter on his lap, he smoothed his fingers across the writing. Anyone else wouldn't be able to differentiate the two, but he could. He had stared at the lettering long enough to notice the slight wobble of the pen in the second letter that the first hadn't had.

Carefully lifting the flap, he eased the envelope open. He couldn't put it off any longer. Cowardice wasn't a part of who he was.

*Dear Gunnar,*

*I know we promised we wouldn't contact each other, that we shouldn't have let what happened in the cabin happen and we need to go back to how it's been since you left for basic.*

*While I had every intention of fulfilling that promise, though it's agony,—*

Gunnar closed his eyes as a wave of pain crashed over him. It shouldn't hurt anymore, being one he'd lived with since he told Julie goodbye. In all the years, it hadn't dulled.

*—what I have to tell you needs to be said.*

*You know those warnings that it only takes one time? Yeah, well, I'm pregnant.*

A whoosh of air rushed out of Gunnar at the news. He had a kid? Why hadn't she said something last night or all day as they worked alongside each other? Guilt forced the indignation out in a cold slap of reality. Of course, she wouldn't say anything. His silence had screamed he didn't care that they had a kid or that she'd needed his help.

*I'm so sorry, Gunnar. I promise I'll do whatever you want regarding our baby. If you still believe we'll be too much of a distraction, your involvement in this baby's life can be as much or as little as you want.*

Vomit pushed up his throat, and he swallowed it down. Had he really been so adamant, so selfish, that she thought he wouldn't want anything to do with their kid?

*But, if you think we might be able to make it work, that you could do your duty to your country and fellow soldiers and have a family, I'll go anywhere you go. I miss you, miss you so much, but I want what's best for you.*

*Love always,*

*Jules*

Questions bottled up within, fighting for answer. Did he have a daughter or a son? What did they look like? They'd be six now. Were they as hardheaded as he had been or the peacekeeper like Julie? Were they here in Fairbanks? Gunnar stood and took a step toward the door. Is that why Julie had acted so skittish the night before and disappeared this morning?

He stopped himself from racing into the frigid night and scouring Fairbanks for them. Demanding an introduction after seven years of abandonment wasn't the way to start a relationship with his kid. He'd had the idiocy to not open the letter when he first got it. Waiting through the night to meet didn't even count as punishment for that sin.

He plopped back on the bed and reached for the other letter that had fallen to the floor. Maybe Julie had found out what they were having and let him know. Not that he deserved even that. He ripped open the envelope, the need to be careful with it evaporating with the need to know.

*Gunnar,*

*I'm sorry. I shouldn't be writing to you, especially when I said I'd leave the decision up to you, but I lost the baby.*

The words blurred as his eyes filled with tears. How could he feel this intense ache of loss? He rubbed his thumb and fingers over his eyes. If he felt this horrible, what had Julie gone through? He should have opened the letters when he first got them, supported her when she needed him most. He forced himself to read the rest.

*When they ran tests to see what happened, they found something. Gunnar, its cancer. Uterine, like what took Mom. Dad's a mess. Saylor too. I'm not much better.*

*The doctors say that losing the baby helped them catch the cancer early enough they think they can treat it. But, I'm scared, so, so scared. I know I shouldn't ask, but I need you.*

*Even if it's just one phone call to hear your voice. You've*
*always talked me through hard times, and I'm not sure I can*
*do this without you. Please, please call.*

    *Love always,*

    *Jules*

    Gunnar's hands shook as her news filled him. He let
the letter drop to the floor, watching his hands tremble.
How could he have let her down? How could he have
been so selfish that the one person who meant the most
to him had to beg for help?

    Help he never gave.

    Rage at himself exploded pain in his head like a dirty
bomb. He roared and chucked his backpack against the
wall. He'd never be able to make it up to Julie, even if he
tried for the rest of his life.

## 10

Julie blinked at the pilot of the third plane they'd chartered like she couldn't understand basic English. "What do you mean 'it won't fit'?"

She glanced from the open side door of the plane to the pile of supplies still needing loaded as a frigid gust of wind whipped her braid against her cheek. She glanced at the stormy sky building to the southwest. This couldn't be happening. She'd done the calculations four times, and, with the winter weather system closing in fast, they didn't have time to mess around.

"You have too much stuff." The pilot waved his hands at the supplies still needing to be loaded.

"I was told I had eighteen thousand pounds, including people." Keeping her voice even stretched her already thin patience.

"Right. You're over. Too fat, honey." He scanned her up and down and winked at her.

Blowing up at the man wouldn't help. Thank goodness Saylor had gone up with the first plane to make sure the base headquarters set-up was going as planned. She'd already have the man whimpering for his mommy, especially since she was already on edge because of the whole Gunnar thing.

Julie forced herself not to look at Gunnar. Not because her possible miscalculation embarrassed her, but because he looked horrible. She'd never, not in all the years she'd known him growing up, would have called him small or frail.

Gladiator? Yes.

Put the statue of David to shame? Absolutely.

Why on this day of all days did he have to be under the weather? Something about the way he held his body when he arrived that morning and the way he'd functioned all day on vacant autopilot gave Julie the impression that he could break. It wasn't comforting, knowing in a matter of days they'd be relying on each other to get across the constantly moving Arctic sea ice.

Mason thought Gunnar was the better person for the team? Julie closed her eyes and let out a slow breath. Of course he was. Even operating at subpar levels, Gunnar would always outperform her.

Didn't mean she had to dwell on that or worry about if he was okay. She pushed her shoulders back and channeled her best Saylor impression. Well, maybe not her best. She could never be as forceful as her cousin. More like a toned-down version, but it had to work on this pilot who was changing the rules.

"I'm not overweight. I've weighed everything twice." Julie crossed her arms over her chest.

"Sorry, honey. Scales don't lie. You're two thousand, nine hundred and thirty-seven pounds over. But don't worry, I can have another plane here in about an hour." The jerk was trying to hustle them.

The downright dirty weasel.

Julie looked away, her anxiety making her fingers numb. How was she going to fix this? They didn't have time to find a different airline, not with the storm blowing in, and even if they did, few companies up here had a big plane like the stripped-down Hawker Siddeley HS 748 this guy had. It was the reason they'd gone with him in the first place. But she didn't want to pay the guy more than they already had.

She rubbed her two fingers up the bridge of her nose to ease the headache building. A touch on her elbow caused her to jump. Gunnar's forehead crinkled in hurt before he smoothed it.

"Can I talk to you?" He tipped his head back to the hangar.

"Yeah." She followed him to the building, trying not to worry about how every step he took looked like he carried the weight of the world on his broad shoulders and it was more than he could handle.

When they got out of the wind, Gunnar turned to her. He glanced at her face, winced, then jerked his attention to the supplies on the tarmac. What the heck was that about? Julie crossed her arms to keep her bruised heart from shuddering. His expressions shouldn't matter anyway, not that her heart got the memo.

"Listen, I have a friend that has a Twin Otter. I texted him, and he can be here in twenty." Gunnar looked at her now, hesitation in his eyes. "That is, if you want him to.

We could also re-weigh everything. Prove this jerk is pulling one over on us."

Her head was shaking before he even finished what he was saying. "There isn't time to re-weigh, not with the storm blowing in. Thank your friend for coming and helping."

He nodded once, then marched into the hangar to make the call. She sighed, both in relief and resignation that Gunnar once again came to the rescue. Now, to let the weasel know he wasn't getting another cent from them.

She approached the pilot, anticipation of his reaction making her heart pound. This guy was trying to cheat them. She shouldn't worry about creating conflict, not with him. Ugh, would she always be such a pushover?

"You can go ahead with the load you have. We've hired another plane that can be here in twenty." She watched his reaction.

His eyes widened in shock, then narrowed in anger.

"We'll call ahead to the team already in Utqiagvik to make sure they're waiting for you at the airstrip to unload." She rushed on, glad Saylor, Mason, Clark, and Sunny had flown the dogs up earlier that morning.

"Fine," the pilot ground out, stomping up the loading ramp. "Pull the stairs away."

He motioned to her with a flick of his wrist. Rolling her eyes, she rushed to the stairs and leaned into them. The wind blew against them, and, with the slick tarmac, she had trouble getting enough force behind her to move them. Gunnar nudged her sideways, bracing his shoulder against one corner. Coming to the rescue again.

"On three." He counted down.

Two people moving the heavy structure was definitely easier than just herself. The hawker powered up before they'd moved out of the way, making her ears hurt from the engine. She and Gunnar got the stairs against the building in time for her to turn and watch the plane rocket down the strip.

Hopefully, the man wouldn't be so upset his ploy didn't work that he sabotaged them. Just the thought made her pulse beat in her throat. She'd have to check all the supplies again just to make sure. She rolled her shoulders at the exhaustion already settling in with the amount of work and time that would take.

"I think I'll check our supplies tonight after they're unloaded." Gunnar sighed, his voice heavy. "I don't trust that man."

"I'll help. I was thinking the same thing." She glanced to the south. The sky darkened more with each second that passed. "Thanks for contacting your friend. If we don't make it before this storm hits, we'll be stuck here for at least three, maybe four days."

"You're welcome." He opened his mouth to say something more, then snapped it shut and went to the pile of supplies.

Forty-five minutes later, she climbed into Gunnar's friend's plane, double-checking the straps holding the crates and boxes down, and sat in the far seat with a sigh. The wind had picked up, but Gunnar's friend had assured her taking off wouldn't be a problem. Gunnar groaned as he climbed into the seat next to her.

"We made it." She sent him a genuine smile as relief rushed through her.

"I knew we would." He rolled his head to her as it rested on his seat. "We make a good team."

Her smile faltered, but she pressed it back into place as she gave him a nod. She turned her gaze out the window as the plane taxied down the runway, her face falling as sorrow replaced relief. They did make a good team, always had. Too bad it wouldn't last.

## 11

J ulie dashed across the street, careful not to slip on the ice. Skipping lunch hadn't been the best idea, but after the mess with the jerk pilot, eating had been the last thing on her mind. Now, she needed food more than a wolverine on a hunt.

Sam & Lee's Restaurant, located three blocks down from the hotel, hopefully was far enough away that no one would venture there. Saylor had wanted her to join her, Clark, and Mason at the restaurant in the hotel, but Julie just wanted to eat, then go hide in her room ... alone.

Yes, hiding never got one far in life. The chance that Gunnar would show up and she'd have to pretend she wasn't watching him when she couldn't help not watching would take too much energy from her. So, she'd told Saylor she just wanted to order dinner in and hit the sack. Then, when loneliness hit, she hauled herself up the street.

Even without the storm making it this far north, cold didn't begin to describe the late February weather in

Barrow—ugh, Utqiagvik. She cringed. Calling this town at the tip of Alaska Barrow was ingrained with years of thinking of it as that. She'd have to keep repeating the Iñupiaq name in her head until it stuck. She didn't want to offend the people of this incredible little town when they'd welcomed them with such excitement.

The locals' help to get the supplies and dogs settled still amazed her. When she and Gunnar had finally landed, the Hawker had already been unloaded and a group of about fifty people milled about, waiting for the last plane to arrive. She knew Mason had been communicating with people here. She just hadn't expected so many.

Mason had also worked with a local musher and built new kennels for the dogs to wait in. The Doggie Motel, as she called it, was nicer than her own set up back in Valdez. She might have a mutiny after she got home, especially after what she and her dogs were about to do.

The breeze blew the enticing smell of burgers and Chinese food to her, making her stomach growl and mouth water. Hopefully, they had some kind of appetizer or something pre-made so she could snack on it while waiting for her dinner. If not, she was so hungry she might invade the kitchen or steal someone else's food. She sprinted the remaining five feet up the ramp to the restaurant's door and yanked it open.

Bright red-and-white-checkered tablecloths covered the tables. The place wasn't busy, which was just what she wanted. Not to be alone, but not to be forced to chat.

"Hello! Sit wherever you like. The seating upstairs has magnificent views." The cheery welcome from an older Asian woman settled Julie's nerves even more.

"Thanks." Julie smiled at the woman and headed to the stairs.

A small group of teenagers sat at a table on the far side of the upstairs, so Julie slid into a booth up against a window on the other side of the room. Noise from the kitchen also located upstairs eased her muscles even more. This was what she needed. People, but not personal.

She stared out the window at the last remnant of sun tinting the horizon light blue against the black night. Even though it was a little after six, sunlight was short at the top of the world in February. Non-existent November through January, so that they would have any light at all on their expedition was a blessing.

One of the hardest parts of planning had been deciding when to leave. The sea ice wouldn't be stable much past mid-April. Even leaving as late as they were pushed it. They might encounter expanses of open water called leads so big they couldn't get across or around. Yet going earlier wouldn't have given them enough light.

"Can I join you?" Sunny's soft question shouldn't have caused Julie to jerk, but it did.

Growing up, the Rebels had all been able to sneak about with a silence that left Julie in awe ... and often screaming like those silly girls in scary movies. Not that she'd ever really watched many of those. Just the commercials gave her nightmares. Sunny, though she was the youngest, had always startled Julie the most. It had been a game for the young girl.

Sunny's lips pressed together like she tried not to laugh. "Sorry. Didn't mean to scare you."

"It's okay. I was lost in thought is all." Julie forced a

smile and pointed at the booth bench across from her. "Have a seat."

While she just wanted to be alone, she couldn't be rude. She'd always loved being around Sunny, even though she was quite a few years younger than Julie. Sunny, with much drama and forcefulness, had once claimed Julie as her best friend. Any time Julie would spend time at the Rebel's homestead, which was several times a week, Sunny wouldn't be far from her side, much to Gunnar's dismay. It had been part of the excitement of going over there, watching Gunnar figure out ways to sneak Julie away so they could spend time alone without an eight-year-old chaperone who loved to blab.

Gunnar's leaving had ruined all that. Well, that wasn't entirely fair. Julie could've continued going over to the Rebels' or had Sunny over to her dad's place that hadn't been far away. Being with the Rebels, knowing that Julie would never be a part of the family she'd loved so much, had been too hard for her. She'd used her father moving them to Valdez as an excuse to cut all ties to the life she'd never have, including the friendship to a spunky little girl.

"Wonder what's good here?" Sunny looked at the menu, shaking Julie from her own thoughts.

She snatched up her menu and scanned the selection. For such a little town past the edge of nowhere, the offerings impressed her. Her stomach growled again, and not a soft rumble. A polar bear could roar next to them and not match the volume her body achieved. Sunny's head shot up, her eyebrows reaching almost to her hairline.

"I don't know, but I might have to order one of everything." Julie smiled and tipped her head to the side.

Sunny burst out laughing. "You think?" She reached into her purse and pushed a box of Lemonheads across the table. "Here, it's not much, but it'll give your stomach something to chew on."

"You still eat these things?" Julie couldn't believe that hadn't changed in all these years.

Sunny had claimed at age five that the candy was full of brightness, just like she was. It had been the only candy she'd eat, and one of the many ways Gunnar would distract her so they could disappear together.

"Guess old habits are hard to break." Sunny shrugged and continued reading the menu.

Tension hung thick in the air between them like fog, not knowing if it wanted to settle in for the day or allow the sun to burn it away. As much as Julie wanted to be alone, she hated that the two of them couldn't be at ease with each other. She'd have to figure out a way to fix that. Traversing the Arctic Ocean and sharing a tent with someone who you couldn't hold a conversation with would add difficulty to the long trip. Julie opened her mouth to ask Sunny about climbing Mount Denali when the waitress interrupted.

"Are you ready to order?" Her friendly gaze bounced between Julie and Sunny, her pen poised above her order pad.

"I'd like the Szechwan spicy chow mein with pork and a piece of pecan pie." Julie closed the menu and held it to the waitress. "Can I get the pie while the meal is cooking, please?"

"No problem." The waitress nodded and turned to Sunny.

"Agh, it all looks so good." Sunny scanned the menu,

flipping it over to read the back again. "Why do you have to have so many choices?"

Her exasperation had Julie laughing.

"It's better than having only a few." She pointed at Sunny and took a drink of her water.

"Yeah, but I want Chinese *and* a burger. I mean, did you see their Barrow Burger? It has ham, cheese, and an egg." Sunny cringed. "How do I decide?"

"Well, we could share." Julie didn't want company, and now she was offering to share?

Would she forever try to make others happy? Did it matter? She'd wanted a burger as well, so splitting benefitted her too.

"Really?" Sunny gave Julie a skeptical look over her menu.

"Sure. I wanted a burger and fries too."

"Okay. I'll take a Barrow Burger, egg over easy, and a piece of cheesecake, please." She closed her menu. "Oh, and bring my dessert first too, please."

"Sounds good." The waitress nodded and headed toward the kitchen.

Sunny gazed out the window, her lips pressed into a slight frown. Julie picked at the paper napkin as the fog of tension that had momentarily lifted settled back between them. She hated the unease. Hated the silence, which was ironic coming from the person who'd five minutes before just wanted to be alone.

"Why didn't you ever come back over after Gunnar left?" Sunny's soft question embedded the discomfort further on Julie's skin, causing her to shiver.

How could she answer that without exposing how broken she'd been? She could just blame it on her dad moving them. That wouldn't explain why she didn't at least write or come by and say goodbye, but it would protect her from having to live through the heartache telling Sunny would create.

Julie looked up from the napkin she'd shredded to confetti, ready to give the lame excuse of moving and change the conversation. The look of distrust on Sunny's face bottled those words in Julie's throat. She couldn't lie, not when this young woman needed the truth.

"I ... I ..."Julie closed her eyes and shook her head. She'd hurt Sunny's feelings more if she lied, so she might as well spit it out. "I couldn't. It was just too hard to be at your place, to be around you all, especially you. Gunnar's leaving had ripped my heart out of my chest. I should have been prepared. I knew it was coming, but I wasn't in a good place." She sighed and shrugged at Sunny. "I guess I'd hoped Gunnar would change his mind. Not about enlisting, but about us. It was a silly hope, but one I'd let in. I loved you all, still do. Wanted to be a part of your family for real. I couldn't handle being with you all, not back then."

"I get that." Sunny bobbed her straw up and down in her glass, her expression still guarded.

"When Dad announced we were moving to Valdez, I tucked tail and ran away with him. Sunny, I'm sorry. I was hurting and selfish. I never should've left things like I did, especially with you."

Sunny moved her glass to the side and reached over to still Julie's hand on her napkin. Her smile was soft and full of compassion. Relief filled Julie and allowed her to breathe, spilling a tear over her lashes.

"I forgive you." Sunny squeezed her hand. "It had to

be hard. I was just so confused why you left me too, but I understand now."

"It wasn't right. I really should've handled that better."

Sunny snorted and rolled her eyes. "No, Gunnar shouldn't have been a complete moron with his 'no distractions' nonsense."

The way she pitched her voice low and gravelly to impersonate Gunnar cracked Julie up.

"He had his reasons." She swept her napkin mess into a neat pile.

"Yeah? Well, now he has nothing." Sunny shook her head, her voice pitching low. "Nothing but a lonely life and a bunch of dogs."

Their desserts arrived, and Julie let the comment go. How could she not? The comment hit way too close to home for comfort, which struck her as ironic ... and more than a little depressing.

## 12

Gunnar trailed after Sunny and the others as they made their way to the press conference. He didn't want to go, had tried to talk his way out of it with more words than he'd strung together in a long time. Mason wouldn't budge, so Gunnar sucked it up.

Situations like these reinforced his reasons for living out of the Seward city limits. He even kept his tours to the minimum needed to make ends meet. Not that he didn't like people. He just didn't like people en mass. He definitely wasn't a fan of a camera shoved in his face and questions peppered at him.

Not that the press would give a rip about him.

He was a nobody.

Keeping that in the front of his mind helped. Kind of. Hopefully, the press would put all their focus on Mason and Sunny, the two superstars of the team, and let him just sit there and observe. Heck, even Julie was a somebody in the mushing circles.

Gunnar needed to talk to her, tell her he was a complete and utter jerk. Wouldn't that be a fun conversation?

*Hey, remember when you sent me those letters telling me you were dying and begging for help? Yeah ... I just opened them, and I'm sorry.*

If Julie didn't slap him in the face, he would. He needed a good right hook to the noggin. Not that it would help. Nothing could make up for how he'd let her down when she'd needed him most.

He ran his fingers over his gritty eyes and rolled his head. Wondering if she was healed, if she was all right now, had kept him up late the last few nights. Not a good thing when he was supposed to be preparing for the expedition.

He stepped into the conference room to lights flashing and too many eyes trained on him. The desire to perform an about-face and double-time it back to his room almost had him moving out the door. Sunny turned and snagged his hand. Her mouthing, "Okay?" proved him a coward.

Pushing his shoulders back, he squeezed her hand and gave a quick nod. He'd jumped from planes into enemy territory in the cover of night, rescued elite special forces teams from dangerous situations, and survived being captured and interrogated by terrorists. He could handle a group of nosy reporters.

Besides, it wasn't like they were covering some breaking news story or anything. They just wanted to get enough for their three-minute segment of the evening news. He could handle thirty minutes of them fawning over Mason and his bigger-than-life personality.

Gunnar pulled out the chair at the table set up at the front of the conference room and forced himself to relax into it. Mason thanked the reporters for coming with a joke about the weather and plunged into his presentation. As he laid out the plan for the expedition, Gunnar breathed a little easier. This wasn't so bad, definitely not worth getting stressed over.

"You all know that Clark and I like to find ourselves a little adventure." Mason laughed at his own joke, causing the reporters to roll their eyes or chuckle with him. "Since we conquered the South Pole, we knew we had to go to the other side of the earth. But we didn't want to just go to the North Pole. A lot of really amazing people have done that, some skiing, some going from Canada unassisted with dog sleds. We thought since that had already been done, why don't we try something new? Why not trek from Alaska to the Pole as fast as possible?"

"Mr. Steele, Katie Cullens here with KUTU. Just how do you plan on doing that? I know Nordic Canine Kibble sponsors racers for the Iditarod and Yukon Quest, but the Arctic Ocean isn't like those terrains. There aren't towns for checkpoints or medical and vet personnel if something goes wrong." The reporter's judgmental tone grated on Gunnar's nerves.

Wasn't Katie Cullens the reporter that tried to corner Bjørn into making the head of search and rescue in Seward look bad? Gunnar clenched his jaw, narrowing his eyes as he observed her expression. Why did she start right in on challenging the expedition? Did she honestly have concerns, or was she just trying to claw her way up the news ladder?

"Great question, Ms. Cullens." The excited tone of

Mason's voice told Gunnar the man ate this attention up. "Each of our team members and their sleds will have GPS trackers on them monitored by our support team here, led by Saylor Reeds of Ascent, Inc. We are taking enough provisions for seven days of travel with three days of emergency rations as back-up. Every sixth day, Saylor and our team of experts will set up our mobile check-point station. Our expedition team will locate it with our GPS trackers that we are taking with us."

"Isn't that risky? The sea ice constantly shifts, and the extreme cold has the propensity to destroy equipment, making it useless." Katie tilted her head, her perfectly shaped eyebrow lifting over her gray eyes.

"That's true, but no glorious adventure comes without danger. Then it wouldn't be an adventure." Mason chuckled, not one bit fazed by her questions. "And to address your point on medical personnel, not only is Clark one of the best physicians in the world, but we are fortunate to have Gunnar Rebel on the expedition, whose experience in the military equipped him to handle any problems thrown our way."

Katie's gaze snapped to Gunnar. Her eyes widened before they narrowed into calculating slits, and Gunnar's skin crawled. Why would she be so interested in him?

Mason continued to discuss the details of the expedition: the other team members, how many dogs each sled had, the ultimate goal. The entire time, Katie's head bent over her phone as she slid her finger across the screen and typed faster than Gunnar had ever seen someone do on a phone. Her smirk right before she lifted her head had dread pooling sweat in his pits.

"Mr. Toll—" Katie interrupted Mason. "I'm confused

by the qualifications you claim Lieutenant Rebel has. This expedition demands expertise in Arctic exploration and dog sledding. Though last summer he took tourists on joy rides across the glaciers in Seward, Mr. Rebel has spent the last fifteen years far from Alaska and the struggles you'll undoubtedly come up against. While his service to our country is commendable, it didn't prepare him for the rigors this expedition will require."

The hackles on Gunnar's neck rose like a wolf defending his position in the pack. Where did this prissy waif of a woman get off saying he wasn't qualified? She had no clue what his qualifications were. Her two minute scour of the internet wouldn't tell her of all the lives he'd saved, the harrowing hours spent putting his life on the line so others could live. He should rip into her, give her a first-hand experience of just a taste of his training.

He clenched his jaw so hard pain exploded behind his eyes. She didn't deserve his justifications. He crossed his arms over his chest and leaned back in his chair. Mason could fill her in if he thought it necessary.

"Excuse me, Katie, right?" Julie's voice was the last one Gunnar expected to hear at that moment, and he whipped his head to her.

"Yes, Katie Cullens with KUTU."

"Well, Katie Cullens with KUTU, do you know what a pararescueman is or the qualifications it takes to become one?" Julie's soft words had Gunnar unfolding his arms and leaning closer.

"No, I don't." The first sign of hesitance entered Katie's tone.

"You question Gunnar's qualifications? He's spent the last fifteen years rescuing Seals and Green Berets. The PJ selection process is the hardest training the US military throws at our soldiers. Less than twenty percent ever finish the two years of rigorous training to become a pararescueman. The military call the PJs in when there isn't any other hope. They're assigned to special ops teams to come up with solutions if and when missions go sideways." With each word Julie spoke in his defense, his eyebrows rose in shock. "Not only that, but Gunnar knows mushing better than most racers I know. He was already an expert at wilderness survival before he went into the Air Force. I can only imagine his training increased his expertise exponentially. Before you so carelessly throw out accusations of inexperience, you really need to do your research. Gunnar Rebel is more than qualified to be a member of this expedition, and I'm grateful to have him on the team."

Julie sat back with a huff, like the rapid release of words exhausted her. Did she really think that, or was she just being the peacekeeper she'd always been? Could it be that she didn't hate his guts for what he had done to her?

She peeked down the table at him and gave a quick lopsided smile and shrug. He nodded his thanks. It was a small movement, not worthy of the gratitude he felt coursing through him. The gratitude zinged right alongside the small measure of hope her defense of him created.

## 13

Julie shoved the key to the high school into the lock, still surprised the superintendent had given the five of them full access to the facilities. He had insisted that they were free to use the pool or gym whenever they wanted. At the time, she hadn't given it much thought except acknowledging how welcoming the community was. Now, when her nervous energy swirled and danced through her veins like the northern lights, she'd be sending the superintendent a big thank you. If she was going to sleep tonight, she had to burn her body to exhaustion, and swimming laps in the pool was the perfect way to do that.

Yanking the door open, she zipped the key back into her purse pocket, made sure the lock latched, then headed down the hall to the pool. Of course, an exhausted body wouldn't matter one iota if her mind refused to shut down. She still couldn't believe she'd come to Gunnar's defense like she had. She didn't do confrontation, especially not with a camera recording every word. Yet, the more that know-it-all reporter had attacked Gunnar, the more Julie snarled.

How was it she and Gunnar had been apart for fifteen years, not counting their one encounter seven years ago, yet she could still read him like she'd always been able to? He could hide his emotions well, but the tightness in his shoulders before they had made their way to the conference room and the slight tick of his cheek and dart of his eyes to the exits as they'd sat at the table screamed his nervousness. She obviously had been paying too much attention to him. Then, when the reporter had started in with her questions pointed at Gunnar and he hadn't corrected the lady, all thoughts of idly sitting by and letting Mason do all the talking flew out the window.

Julie had felt Gunnar's gaze on her as her words had tumbled out faster than her brain could think. His shock and gratitude when she'd dared to glance at him settled the protectiveness that had roared through her into a contented purr in her core. She groaned as the warm feeling returned with just the thought of him and his piercing brown eyes.

How could she still have that reaction after everything that had happened? Yeah, right. Lying to herself never got her anywhere. She'd never stopped loving Gunnar, even when she'd been in relationships with others. Wasn't that why she was alone? Saylor thought it was Julie's inability to trust again, which she supposed was partly true.

But the bigger truth, the one Julie had kept inside all these years, was that she still saw his face when she closed her eyes.

Still felt his fingers slide through her hair.

It wouldn't be fair to start a relationship with anyone else when she still longed for another. Saylor would keel over dead, then come back to haunt Julie if she ever told her cousin. So, Julie kept it all inside. No need to throw Saylor into a conniption over it when there was no chance of changing the status quo.

Only ... now there was a chance, wasn't there?

Julie leaned her shoulder against a trophy case and closed her eyes with a shake of her head. Thoughts like that wouldn't help her sleep. Thoughts like that wouldn't help her, period.

Just because Gunnar suddenly showed up, didn't mean they could start right back where they'd left off. Even if he was interested, she didn't want that. The memory of how cherished she'd felt in his arms flitted through her mind, calling her a liar ... again.

She gritted her teeth and stomped toward the pool.

Memories and longings didn't matter.

Reality did.

Getting her hopes up that a future waited for her and Gunnar would only lead to more heartache. For both their sakes, she'd leave the past in the past, the good and the bad. She had promised to always be his friend. This expedition was the perfect proving ground for that promise.

Stashing her clothes in the locker room, she snagged the hotel towel and rushed out toward the pool. The sooner she got in the water, the quicker she could work herself to exhaustion. She needed sleep if she was going to be in top shape before they left.

Soft splashes echoed in the cavernous room, drawing her attention to the water. Gunnar glided through the water with sure, smooth strokes, flipped at the opposite wall, then rocketed back toward her. With a groan, her shoulders slumped, though her heart skipped like a startled squirrel, then pounded as fast as excited squirrel chatter.

The universe hated her.

Or God had a twisted sense of humor.

Resigned to the fact that Gunnar wouldn't be getting out of her head soon, she tossed her towel on the bench next to his and sat on the edge of the pool. She dangled her legs in the water, trying to ignore the increase in her pulse as each stroke brought him closer. Not once did his pace falter. Did he realize she was here? Maybe it'd be better to slip away and let him do his laps in peace.

About halfway across, he disappeared under water. She searched, waiting for him to pop up like a seal, probably on the opposite side, far from her. He came into view, swimming along the bottom of the pool directly toward her.

She clenched her hands around the smooth concrete edge. Her chest weighed a ton as she tried to take a deep breath of chlorine-thick air and calm down. The closer he got, the harder it was to breathe.

This was a mistake.

She should just leave.

No. Avoiding him would only last so long. It'd be better to get this awkwardness over now before they were fighting for their lives on the sea ice.

Gunnar skimmed up the side of the pool. For a second, she thought he'd grab her ankle and pull her in like he used to. She pressed her lips together to stifle the ridiculous disappointment when he didn't.

He broke the surface, water cascading down his head. It really wasn't fair that he still looked like some sea god. If merpeople existed, he'd be their king. He wiped a hand down his face and held on to the side of the pool with the other.

The heaviness of being here with him, of seeing him healthy and alive after so many years of wondering, threatened to push her into the water and drown her. She'd been a fool to think she'd ever get over him, but he didn't need the tension that her inability to move on would cause.

He already struggled around others. She could tell by the way he always looked like a jack-in-the-box coiled too tight. Something had happened to him while he was deployed. Maybe lots of somethings. Which made sense, given how changed he now was. He'd never been as outgoing as Sunny, but he'd always found enjoyment around others. Now, it seemed like a struggle. Even here, with just the two of them, his shoulders bunched like he was ready to bolt.

No. She wouldn't make things harder on him. Keeping her feelings bottled up hadn't killed her over the last fifteen years. What would another few weeks—at the most, a month—more hurt?

"Hey." She forced a smile. "Can't sleep?"

"Rarely. You?" He finally looked at her, and she swallowed the pain lodged in her throat his concerned gaze caused.

"Nope." She took a deep breath, letting his comment of not sleeping go, and pointed her chin at the pool. "Nice that we can come here instead of being stuck pacing the hotel room."

"Yeah." He glanced over his shoulder at the pool.

Would he talk more than just a word at a time? Did she really want him to? It wasn't like they had a ton to talk about. At least, not without bringing up the past.

He sighed like it came all the way from his toes. With no effort at all, he hoisted himself out of the water and sat next to her. Water sloshed from him, chilling her legs, but she didn't care.

*Please don't leave.*

The fear that he would stand up and say good night hit her like an icy tsunami. No, no, no. She pulled her top lip between her teeth and bit hard. She couldn't let her feelings for him overwhelm her. Not again. She'd barely survived the last time.

She was different now. Staring down death changed her, made her stronger. Resilient. If she could live through that, she could exist within a friendship with Gunnar.

"You ready for tomorrow?" Maybe if she kept things on neutral ground, the next time they were together wouldn't be so tense.

"Guess so." He shifted next to her, and she forced herself to look at him. "I'm still catching up to the idea that we get to go."

She skimmed her gaze along his defined muscles as they flexed and relaxed. Geesh. He'd been in shape before. The military had honed all those angles that had driven her crazy as a teen into something truly swoon-worthy. She curled her toes through the water and forced her gaze to his face.

"Yeah. Me too, and I've had almost a year to get used to the idea." Her attention snagged on a scar that started at his ear and trailed down his neck and over his shoulder. "Oh, Gunnar. What happened here?"

She touched his neck with her fingertips. The ridge of the scar and his cool, damp skin shot tingles up her fingers through her arm. Her hand trembled as she pulled it away and curled it around the pool's edge.

"Nothing." He touched where she just had.

"Okay."

She understood his reluctance to tell her. He didn't have to talk about his time away. Her asking was selfish and put him on the spot.

"Sorry, Jules. I'm still not used to talking about it." Gunnar shook his head, taking a deep breath. "When a rescue mission went sideways, I had a little campout with some terrorists who wanted me to chat about things they couldn't know."

Tears burned hot and sudden in her eyes, making her nose sting. "They tortured you?" The words hurt as she forced them past the boulders in her throat.

"Not bad." He shrugged and rubbed his hand across a scar on his stomach that looked like burn marks. "The cavalry swooped in before they could do any real harm."

She swallowed, blinking the tears away before they fell. If he didn't want to make a big deal about it, she wouldn't either. Yet, she scanned his body again, noticing scars here and there. Some looked like bullet holes, others like more knife slashes. All reminded her of the fear she'd lived with, not knowing if he was safe or not.

The tattoo across his shoulder and down his arm snagged her attention. The realism of the American flag impressed her, but the PJ motto inked in the bright red stripes drove home Gunnar's mission in life. *These things we do, that others may live.* He'd always been willing to sacrifice himself for others.

That wouldn't stop just because he was home.

He took a deep breath, like he needed to prepare himself. She tore her gaze from the words inked on his bicep and braced for what he wanted to say.

"The other day, after Saylor blew up, I ... I read your letters." He turned his tear-filled eyes to her. "Jules, I'm so, so sorry." He dropped his chin to his chest, like his head was too heavy to hold.

He hadn't known?

Hadn't even read the letters?

That heaviness that had settled on her built in her chest like a musk ox had trampled her. She sucked in a breath, letting it shake out as the other part of his words sunk in.

"You still had them?" Her head spun as she looked at him for answers. "Why?"

"Selfishness. No, cowardice." He ground out, cursing beneath his breath. "And to think all these years they comforted me."

"What do you mean?"

"I'm such a fool and a jerk. I thought you'd written to tell me you missed me. That you loved me." He huffed a humorless laugh. "I'd lie with those letters on my chest when I couldn't sleep, imagining the words you wrote. Remembering little details of you. They were my freaking security blanket."

Julie didn't know what to say. Her body had gone numb with the news he hadn't even read her letters. She couldn't stand and walk away if she tried. Yet, that her letters, that thoughts of her, had gotten him through his difficult days had her stomach flip-flopping so violently she might throw up.

"I should've known that something was wrong. Should've known you wouldn't contact me if it wasn't important." His knuckles turned white as he gripped the side of the pool. "Me and that stupid, selfish promise."

"It wasn't stupid. You needed to focus on your missions." She took a deep breath, holding it until her courage filled her. "I'm ... I'm glad you didn't read them. Glad they helped you."

"You needed me, and I failed you. Not once, but twice."

"I lived, learned just how strong I was. Learned how to depend on myself and not others. I wouldn't have done that if you'd been there." She skimmed her fingers along the PJ motto, making his bicep jump. "We both had to sacrifice, but what you did, all the men and women you saved, they were worth it."

He shook his head. As she dropped her fingers, he snagged them, rubbing his thumb along their tips. He swallowed so hard she heard it.

"You're okay now?" Fear for her blazed in his eyes.

"Yeah. Healthy as an ox." She smiled, wanting more than anything to ease his guilt. "Race you."

She dived into the pool and took off for the other side. Saylor would call her an idiot, and maybe Julie was. Sure, she'd always been the peacemaker, but her cancer had proved that life was too short to hold on to hurt.

## 14

Gunnar rode back to the hotel in the taxi with Julie. How in the world could she forgive him after what he'd done? Guilt ate at him, calling him a coward. He never would have associated that word with himself before. It fit.

When it came to Julie, he was terrified. Instead of facing his fear, he'd always ran. Pushed her away. Promised, for the good of the many, that they had to "sacrifice."

That word ate at him just as much as the guilt. Leaving her behind, cutting all ties, hadn't been a sacrifice. It'd been a panicked retreat. One that cost both of them. He glanced at her across the backseat. It'd cost her more than him.

He didn't deserve her forgiveness. Not by a long shot. But he'd do everything he possibly could to not let her down again. How he would manage that, he wasn't sure. If the Air Force gave him nothing else, it gave him the keen ability to solve problems. He just hoped he could hone that skill for fixing their friendship.

The car pulled up to the curb. As he pushed the door open, the wind whipped the handle out of his hand. This would be a beast to deal with tomorrow when they took off for the North Pole if it didn't let up.

"Wind's bad." He touched Julie's hand to stop her from opening her door, then snatched it back. "Slide out here."

She scooted toward him, and he thanked the driver before getting out. He stood next to the car, blocking as much of the wind as he could from hitting her. One good gust and Julie would be down the block.

"This better blow over before tomorrow, or the reporters won't be happy." Julie hiked her bag up on her shoulder, tucked her head, and beelined for the door.

Her soft squeak sounded a moment before her arms pinwheeled. Gunnar wrapped his arm around her waist, shifting his own feet as they slipped beneath him. The wind battered them, yanking his feet out from under him. They were going down.

He twisted as they fell and pulled Julie close to his chest. The unyielding concrete slammed into his back. He grunted as she landed on top of him and the air whooshed from his lungs. She was safe. That was all that mattered. Her body shook as her giggles floated through the air.

She pushed her hands against his chest to peer down at him. The soft peach light from the streetlamp haloed her, throwing shadows on her face and making her blush stand out on her cheeks. A strand of her chestnut hair had escaped from under her hood and tickled his cheek where the wind teased it.

Man, seeing her hurt.

Not in the this-is-going-to-suck hurt, though it might. No, this pain was the kind that cut away infection. The sharp, stabbing burst opened the dying part of himself in the way that made him think he might actually find wholeness again.

He lifted his hand and slid the strand of hair behind her ear, rubbing his thumb across her cheek in the process. If he cupped his fingers around her neck, he could pull her in and taste the lips he'd dreamed about for more years of his life than not. Her gaze dipped to his mouth, ratcheting his desire up to new levels. He wanted to give in, to promise her he'd never let her down again.

The wind pummeled them, dousing him with frigid reality. He couldn't be promising her anything. Not with how colossally he'd screwed up last time.

"You okay?" He sat up, lifting her with him.

"You took the brunt of that fall. Are you okay?" She scrambled off his lap to stand.

Holding his hands on her hips until she had her footing firm, he tried to keep his mind off of how good it felt to have her near. To touch her, even with layers of winter gear on. She'd always been calming to him, his eye within the storm. She hooked her bag across her chest, then reached her hand down to help him up.

"Peachy." He shook his head at her hand and eased onto his feet.

He didn't want to take the chance of pulling her down. After getting his footing, he wrapped his hand around her elbow and headed for the entrance. They both stomped their feet when they got inside, and the front desk attendant looked up from her book.

"Sidewalk's slick." Gunnar pointed his thumb over his shoulder. "Needs sand."

"Oh, I'm sorry. I hope you weren't hurt." The employee set her book down and glanced past them to the doors. "I'll get someone to take care of that right away."

"Thanks." Gunnar's reply had Julie peeking up at him.

Her eyes sparkled, and a smile played at her mouth. What did she find so amusing? He thought back over his words but couldn't figure out what could possibly be funny. They got into the elevator, and she still fought to keep her lips from smiling.

"What?" He nudged her arm with his elbow. "What's funny?"

"Nothing."

"Something is." He turned so he could face her.

After fifteen years conjuring her in his mind, he wanted to stare at her. Find all the little things that had changed and memorize them. Like the small scar along her right cheekbone or the few crinkles next to her eyes.

"It's not funny. Not really. It's just your ability to string as few words together as possible and still get the point across is commendable." She peeked up at him and let her smile go.

It would be so easy to lean down and kiss her. The desire to do just that raged up within him, so he shrugged and stepped to the door as it dinged open. She may smile at him now, her peacemaker's heart wanting to ease the tension between them, but he could almost guarantee she didn't want him anymore.

"Talking's overrated." He shrugged.

"So, you truly believe actions speak louder than words?" She matched his step as they walked down the hall.

"Maybe." Though he didn't like what his past actions said about him.

"Hmm. Interesting." Her right eyebrow lifted, her gaze up at him calculating. "Welp, this is me."

She stopped in front of her room and rocked back on her heels. Her eyes darted across the hall to where Gunnar knew Saylor's room was. Did Julie worry her cousin would yank the door open and storm at him again? He deserved it and more. Could even let her get some good punches in, though knowing Saylor, it'd torque her noodle that he wanted her to.

Julie dropped her eyes to the floor and took a step closer, making Gunnar's pulse fire rapidly in his neck like an M249 gun. "I'm really glad you're back home and safe." She peeked up at him and about did him in. "One less worry for me."

She shouldn't have had a single thought of him beyond what a jerk he was, yet she'd feared for him. He needed to retreat before he did something she opposed later when reality slammed back on her, like bend down and kiss her.

He shoved his hands in his coat pockets so he wouldn't reach for her and took a step back, not missing the disappointment that flashed in her eyes. "Me too."

Glad he would be on this expedition with her. Glad he could keep her safe in the extreme conditions to come. But more than anything, he was glad she'd survived the battle she'd waged against cancer. That he could be near her, to be enveloped in the peace that filtered into those around her ... even if it was just for the next few weeks.

Gunnar growled low at the circus the expedition launch had turned into. Too bad the wind had died down, and the sun glared brightly from the southern horizon. Maybe then what should have been an organized rollout wouldn't have turned into the Mason Steele show.

Gunnar glared at the reporters still peppering Mason with questions as Gunnar checked the straps holding down the gear in his sled. Maybe he was being too harsh. He liked Mason. Respected the man and all he'd done. But all this fanfare grated on Gunnar, making him nervous.

Distractions bred mistakes.

Mistakes lost lives.

Wasn't that what he'd drilled into himself so many years ago? Just because he wasn't dodging bullets didn't mean those statements weren't still true. The Arctic sea didn't give a rip about one's celebrity status. The next

1,301 miles to the North Pole would take constant vigilance to get all five of them and the dogs home safely.

Gunnar stared out across the vast white that stretched before them. What if that Katie Cullens chick was right? Most of the last fifteen years he'd been in the Middle East sandbox from hell or the sweltering jungles of Hades. Rarely had a mission taken him to the farthest tips of the hemispheres. What if he couldn't keep everyone safe? Couldn't anticipate trouble and work around it? Maybe it was a mistake for him to come along.

Glancing over at the others, Gunnar squinted at Mason's dogs. They lunged against the leads, anticipating the departure that should've happened already if Mason wasn't so consumed with landing on the evening news. Gunnar didn't like the way they were ratcheting up their excitement. All the dogs were riled up.

Yet, they all had to wait, since Mason wanted to lead the charge. Being the majority funder for the expedition gave him the say in that. It didn't give him the right to let down his guard, though.

"Can we go already?" Sunny yelled behind him, her exasperation mirroring his own.

Gunnar turned around and cupped his hands over his mouth to be heard above the noise. "Celebrities."

Sunny rolled her eyes and shook her head.

As Gunnar turned back to get them moved out, Mason's lead dogs lunged hard against their traces, dislodging the snowhook from the ice. The sled jerked out of Mason's hand, almost toppling him. Gunnar stomped on his hook to reinforce it and motioned to a local to hold his sled. If they didn't catch Mason's team, who knew how far the dogs would go in their current state of mind?

Instead of jetting off across the sea, the dogs veered to Julie's dog team, just ahead and to the side of them. Gunnar shouted and sprinted across the ice as snarls and angry barking filled the air. Julie rushed into the middle of the dogfight, pushing the animals apart, and Gunnar's heart nearly exploded in his chest. Those dogs could turn on her in an instant.

Grabbing dogs by the harness, he yanked and pulled them apart. Mason finally clued in to something other than himself and helped. When the two sleds were separated and Clark was helping Mason move his sled away, Gunnar turned to Julie and stepped close. She bent over her lead dog that had gotten the brunt of the attack and examined his flank.

"You okay?" Gunnar crouched by the next dog in line and looked him over.

Julie huffed out a sigh of relief, patting her lead dog on the side. "We're good."

"That shouldn't have happened." He jerked to standing, stepping closer.

Pulling her hood off, she yanked her mittens back on. "There's just a lot of excitement right now. Things will settle down once we're on the ice."

He shook his head, not believing what she'd said. Her dogs could've been injured. She could've been attacked. And it was okay?

Heck no.

If they were going to survive this expedition, they all had to be on one hundred percent all the time.

"Gunnar, really." Julie placed her hand on his arm.

"It's okay. All of this, all these people, are here to be a part of something amazing. Mason is giving them that, the chance to be a part of history. Once we get going, he'll focus."

Gunnar put his hand over hers. "You could've been hurt."

Her smile at him nearly took him to his knees. "I've been breaking up dog fights since I was five. This was an easy fix."

"Everyone okay?" Mason sucked in air as he approached.

"Yeah," Julie answered as Gunnar shook his head and clenched his teeth.

He should just let it go. Get on the trail and forget it ever happened. Years of vigilance and focused dedication wouldn't allow him to leave it be.

"What are you doing?" Gunnar dropped his voice so the people gathered around wouldn't hear. "The expedition starts now, not after we leave this crowd. Not when we get past this first easy stretch and hit pressure ridges. Now. Your lack of diligence could've cost Julie and your dogs, and then where'd your expedition be?"

"Gunnar, it's all right." Julie's hand was back on his arm as Mason stared Gunnar down.

"No, it's not all right. Either get your head in the game or call the whole thing off, Steele." Gunnar stomped to his team without waiting for an answer, rolling the tension off of his shoulders.

Katie Cullens stepped into his path. Her perfectly styled hair and trendy coat looked out of place among the well-bundled mass. She had to be freezing.

"Not the best way to start an expedition, Lieutenant

Rebel." The way she threw his rank around rankled. "Do you think this indicates the success of the expedition?"

What kind of question was that? If he could push past her, he would. Her chin shivered, and a vulnerability flashed in her eyes before she pressed her lips together to stop the motion. Fine. He'd cut her some slack this time.

"No. The dogs are just excited to get going. Happens." Gunnar shrugged and stepped around her.

She wasn't having any of his brush off, though. Blocking his way again, she flashed a fake smile at him.

"Do you think the hype surrounding the expedition has the team members distracted?" She glanced point-edly at Mason, then lifted her eyebrows when she returned her gaze to Gunnar.

"This expedition's success will be historic. Mason understands that, and he wants all those here, all the people who've supported us locally and our base team, to know that they are a part of history. I'm not worried about his focus and neither should you."

With that, Gunnar pushed past Katie with a nod and ignored her call of his name. He'd have to thank Julie for giving him words to get the reporter off his back. Hopefully, he wouldn't have to talk to Katie Cullens again. Ever would be even better.

The string of words was exhausting. The press of people wore on him. When Mason waved to the crowd and hollered at his dogs to get up, all of Gunnar's tension rushed from his body as his dogs raced after the other four teams.

## 16

Julie added more snow to the pot balanced over the compact camp stove. The hiss filled the small tent she'd be sharing with the Rebels for the unforeseeable future. She'd had trouble lighting the small propane unit, more so than the slightly larger one just outside heating water for the dogs. The negative thirty temperatures hadn't been the regulator's friend. After a lot of grumbling, knocking of metal, and finally shoving the cankerous piece in her coat to warm it up, she'd finally gotten the thing to light.

Doubt had clawed up her shoulder, whispering her shortcomings, as she'd fumbled with the pieces of the stove, trying to figure out what was wrong. Everyone on the team had jobs, and, while they all differed in their physical requirement, every single one of them essential for the success of the expedition. If she couldn't get the stoves to work, they couldn't water the dogs, prepare their food, or heat the tent.

The relief at hearing the fuel ignite had tears threatening to spill. Since the dogfight earlier, she'd questioned her qualifications for being on the team. Gunnar had recognized the problem before chaos had exploded. Her father would have too. What had she been doing? Not paying attention while she griped in her head at Mason to get the show on the road. She should've been yelling at herself to keep her head on straight, not moaning about Mason and his long-windedness.

She blinked the tears from her eyes, scrubbing them with a piece of cloth to wipe away any moisture, and slid her goggles back over her eyes. The tent's door flapped with the wind as she unzipped it and crawled out. She still had one more team of dogs to water before she could settle in for the night. While she didn't need the goggles to protect from the reflection of the sun against the snow anymore, she didn't want any moisture her silly tears might have left on her skin freezing in the frigid wind.

After watering the last team, she carefully brought the extra stove into the tent, where it would stay warmer and hopefully be easier to light in the morning. The heat from the littler stove hit her as she crawled back inside. She'd have to take her parka off, or she'd be sweating. The last thing she wanted was her clothes or gear to get soaked with moisture this early in the game. Condensation would be a constant concern with sweating and, in the tent, simply breathing. The longer she could avoid ice building up in the layers of her gear, the warmer she'd stay.

Sunny sat at the stove, feeding it with more snow. Steam curled white above three mugs on the ground next to her. The rich, smoky aroma of salmon chowder filled the air, and Julie's stomach rumbled.

Slipping off her boots and tucking them in the corner, Julie crawled onto her sleeping bag. Tent walls lightly flapping in the wind, she grabbed her pack from the sleeping bag next to her and propped it behind her for a backrest. The cramped space closed in around her, and she had the temptation to go sleep on her sled. The tight quarters would get even tighter when Gunnar finished securing the rest of the supplies.

She glanced to her left, then right, wondering how she drew the first sleeping-in-the-middle straw. Being in the tent with Gunnar would be hard enough, given how she'd practically thrown herself at him the night before and he'd walked away. Being curled up right next to him would be torture. She'd rather sleep frozen to the tent walls. Or better yet, snuggling with her dogs outside.

"I can't tell you how thankful I am you brought Heather's Choice backpacking meals." Sunny inhaled the aroma from the mug she held, then passed it to Julie.

"Her stuff is the best." Julie wrapped her chilled hands around the warm container and sighed at the instant relief. "I'm glad I talked her into being a sponsor. This chowder is to die for."

"Oh man, and the African Peanut Stew? Mmm, mmm, mmm." Sunny closed her eyes and did a little dance with each moan. "I love meat, like eat-it-every-meal *love* it. But after eating that vegan stew, I bought two cases of it to have at home. So ... good."

The zipper for the door opened, and Gunnar climbed in. His mouth twitched up in a smile, and excitement lined his eyes. His shoulders had relaxed since they'd left the crowds on the shore and ventured across the frozen ocean. He was totally in his element and loving it.

And dang it if he didn't look sexy as all get out doing so.

Nothing would ever prepare Julie for seeing him every day like this. She focused on the chowder cradled in her hands and took a slow, methodical bite. If she could just keep her attention elsewhere, maybe she could guard her heart and not embarrass herself. Yet, she hated the discomfort that pushed the easy atmosphere she and Sunny had created.

"Dinner done?" Gunnar's two words had her smiling into her mug.

"Yep, and you're in for a treat." Sunny placed one more lump of snow in the pot, turned so her back was to the stove, and pointed at the dinner. "Julie got us Heather's Choice."

"Yeah?" His eyes darted to Julie, one attractive eyebrow lifting in question.

He really needed to tone down the appeal. Not that he could actually do that. Which meant Julie needed to control her sudden lovesickness. She shouldn't even be afflicted with it, not after all their relationship went through. Too bad the image of him stretched out in a makeshift barrack after a grueling day, her letters pressed against his chest in comfort, kept bombarding her mind.

She cleared her throat. "It's an Alaskan company that creates these tasty freeze-dried meals."

"Nothing like those nasty military surplus MREs you eat." Sunny pretended to gag. "Those things have so many preservatives in them, I'm surprised you don't glow in the dark."

"They fill me up." Gunnar shrugged, then took off his parka.

Four words this time. Could they get him to say more? Julie shivered as she looked at Gunnar sitting there in a lightweight jacket. The little stove couldn't have warmed the tent above zero, and here he was in half the clothes she had on. Even when they were younger, he'd always ran hot. She didn't think she'd be warm until they made it back to solid land.

"That's about all they do. You'll be eating like a king on this trip." Sunny pointed her spoon at him. "In fact, I bet you'll throw all the MREs you have stashed at the cabin away when we get home."

Gunnar snorted. "Doubtful."

Nuts.

They were back to one-word sentences.

Julie finished her soup, the heat pooling in her stomach. She gave a satisfied sigh, and Gunnar trained his gaze on her. He scanned her like he searched for injury. The action stirred her, turning the chowder into bubbling lava that rolled languidly through her veins the longer he looked at her.

She unzipped her parka with a jerk. The tent suddenly sweltered. She folded her parka on top of her pillow and adjusted her jacket. She wanted to take that off, too, but knew the temperature still wasn't anywhere above zero in their arctic cocoon.

Sunny smirked as her eyes bounced between the two of them. "Welp, we got pretty far today considering how long it took us to get out of town."

"Yep." Gunnar took a bite of his chowder, his eyes widening.

"Told you," Sunny taunted.

Icy chunks of emotion clogged Julie's throat. She'd

missed these two so much over the years. Missed the way she'd always felt being around them. Though years separated her and Gunnar from Sunny, they'd always gotten along so well. Julie opened her thermos and took a long drink of the lukewarm water. It didn't wash the loneliness lodged in her throat away, but at least she could talk.

"It would've been nice to start earlier, but our pace once we left was decent." She pulled her pack into her lap. "Once we hit pressure ridges, we'll probably be measuring our gains in feet rather than miles."

The jumbles of ice and snow pushed up by the constant movement of water worried her the most about the expedition. The daunting and constantly shifting barriers would be treacherous to climb over, especially with the dogs and sleds. Of course, the leads of open water that could appear out of nowhere wouldn't be a walk in the park, either.

Julie took a deep breath to slow her ramping heartbeat and opened her pack. She knew what she had been getting into when she agreed to be a part of the team. Letting the fears of what was to come run rampant through her mind would only make her miserable. She reached her hand into her pack and pulled out the bag full of frozen homemade donuts she'd brought.

"You didn't." Gunnar's low rumble startled a smile from her.

He'd always loved her grandma's donuts. Bringing a dozen every trip they had taken in high school had been one of her favorite ways to show Gunnar she'd loved him. Freezing them and warming them over the fire had been a trick her father used when racing. Said it was the best treat after a long day in the cold. Dad had been right, but she never would have admitted the real treat was Gunnar's reaction when she pulled them out.

"I did." She handed him two, their fingers brushing as he took them.

"I dreamed about these donuts while deployed, about biting into their warm sweetness." He twisted them in his hands, studying them like they were some sort of treasure instead of a pastry. "Especially when we were trapped somewhere without supplies."

Julie cleared her throat, amazed how thoughts of something they'd once shared had been a memory he hadn't forgotten. "In that case, I'm glad I made a ton and have Saylor bringing more at each checkpoint."

He smiled up at her, a smile unfettered with the restraint he'd had up to then. Maybe having this adventure with him wouldn't be as awkward as she thought. Her gaze slipped to his lips before she yanked it down to the bag of donuts. Then again, if she kept ogling him and imagining kissing him senseless, the next few weeks would be the longest of her life.

## 17

Gunnar glanced at his watch and tucked it back into his sleeping bag with a silent groan. One in the morning, and he hadn't slept a wink. In the Air Force, he'd learned the uncanny ability of falling asleep in an instant, no matter where he was.

Sunny called it his superpower.

He called it survival.

Whatever.

The power had escaped him at the worst possible time. All because of the incredible woman lying next to him. Her ability to forgive and let the past go floored him. Not only that, but the easy camaraderie they'd shared in the tent went far beyond forgiveness.

Her extending friendship to him after what he'd done to her had all kinds of warm feelings jumbling up his brain. Those feelings created a constant reel of possibilities repeating through his imagination. Those thoughts, combined with her being right next to him, were his kryptonite.

Would sleeplessness plague him for the entire expedition? His body could go a solid seventy-two hours without sleep. Of course, that had been during hell week and intense missions that didn't allow the luxury of rest, not when there were hours each night of nothing. Plus, his body would go into repair mode when the mission was over, and he wouldn't wake for hours. That couldn't happen here. The only thing that would keep them from moving forward to the North Pole would be injury or blizzard. He wasn't about to be the one keeping them behind.

Julie blew out a shuddering breath next to him, and he rolled on to his side to face her. Her sleeping bag rustled, then her teeth chattered. He drew his eyebrows together as his muscles bunched.

Shoot.

She was cold. She always was cold. Some things never changed. His lip twitched. She even wore her parka to bed.

He fisted his hands around his sleeping bag. In the past, he'd unzip his bag and pull her into his, her bag and all. She'd bury her face into his neck and sleep deeply while he roasted, but it had been worth every second.

Now?

Well, he could scoot up next to her. Their combined body heat might warm her up. She couldn't get mad at him for being close, right? There wasn't much room in the tent to begin with.

He rolled his eyes at his idiocy and slid over so the pressure of her curled up body pressed against him. Her sigh and relaxation had all kinds of delusions of super hero status puffing up his chest. His body mass helped her stay warm. So what? Anyone could do that for her.

In fact, she'd probably stay much warmer sandwiched between Mason and Clark in the other tent. If she kept freezing each night, Gunnar would suggest it. He'd hate every word that came from his mouth and probably would sleep less than if she were here with him, but at least she'd be warmer.

She shivered next to him. It would be so easy to open his sleeping bag and drag her in with him like he'd always done. Every nerve and muscle screamed for him to protect her.

Love her.

Not that his loving her ever stopped. Nope. Fifteen years later and she still filled his thoughts when he had nothing to keep him busy.

She still haunted his dreams at night. She was there, in the midst of his ugliness, running on the battlefield, searching. The counselor helping Gunnar through his PTSD said it was normal for his civilian life and war life to merge in his subconscious. It sucked seeing her there. Even in the nightmares, he tried to protect her, running flat out through pinging bullets to get to her. Always taking too long.

Could she have been in his dreams because he'd let her down in real life? Had his subconscious been trying to tell him to stop taking the coward's way out by not opening her letters? Not protecting her when she needed it most?

Julie shivered again, and Gunnar pushed his nightmares aside. He couldn't tumble down that rabbit hole, not if he wanted to keep his focus. He may have let her down before, but he wouldn't again.

The question remained, did he ask her if she wanted to share the warmth of his bag? He wanted to finally hold her close. To take the second chance he saw in her eyes when she looked at him.

He didn't deserve it. Not after what he'd done. But wasn't that the whole point of mercy? Unmerited kindness and caring?

Proving to Julie that he'd be there for her, that he'd keep his first promise he'd made to her in high school, needed to come before he could rightfully ask to hold her in his arms. With that realization firmly in his mind, he reached up and snagged his parka from the hook dangling from the tent's hangloop. He carefully spread the coat on top of Julie and scooted more firmly alongside her. For now, that would have to be enough.

J ulie groaned and curled further into the ball she'd rolled into. She wasn't shivering, praise the Lord, but her entire body ached from the cold. She'd lost count of how many times she'd woken up frozen to her core. One would think after more than twenty years of mushing, that she'd be used to the cold. During the day, she was constantly on the move and the temperature didn't get to her as badly. Nights were miserable, though.

No matter.

She'd eventually fallen asleep, so she shouldn't whine, even if the big baby session was only in her head. Stretching out in her bag, she let another groan out and buried her head deeper into the cover pulled up to her face. Why did it smell like Gunnar and rush all kinds of memories into her morning brain fog?

Slowly emerging from the cocoon, she blinked to focus her eyes to the light and narrowed her eyes at

Gunnar's parka clutched in her fingers. Her heart swelled in her chest as she pulled it up to her nose and breathed in his scent that reminded her of the outdoors and happier days.

She opened her eyes and found him feeding snow to the pot with a satisfied smirk on his face. Had he seen her sniffing his coat like a lovesick dog?

"Good morning." She might as well get going.

Hanging out in her sleeping bag all day wasn't an option, especially when they had good weather. There might be days ahead with them stuck inside if a storm blew in. Then, she'd have all the time in the world to make a fool of herself.

"Morning." Gunnar smiled at her.

It was the one where only one side of his mouth hitched up. Oh, how she wanted to press her lips against that lift. *That* would make this morning good. Why shouldn't she? Because she wouldn't be the first one making a move, that's why.

Right?

Maybe.

Her reasons for keeping her distance made little sense now.

"Thanks." She sat up and handed the parka to him.

"You were shivering. I wanted to help." Gunnar slid his fingers along hers as he took the coat. "You've always been so cold."

His low voice and warm touch tumbled excitement into her stomach like a litter of wrestling puppies. Memories of how he used to pull her close to warm her up flooded her cheeks with burning heat.

Great.

Not only had he caught her sniffing his coat. Now, her cheeks were broadcasting his effect on her. The last thing she wanted was to make their circumstance uncomfortable for him.

"Coffee?" Gunnar went back to tending the pot.

"Definitely."

She crawled out of the sleeping bag and got to work rolling it up, grateful Sunny had taken the first morning watering the dogs. Julie loved that about being part of a team rather than how she normally dogsledded. They all worked together and took turns with jobs. That few minutes of extra time in the morning could be what helped keep their spirits up.

When she finished packing her gear, she worked on stowing Sunny's sleeping bag. Team spirit brimmed from Julie, giving her a delightful buzz. Maybe she needed to find a way to continue dog sledding but not in such a solo atmosphere.

"Here." Gunnar extended a steaming mug to her. "Two sugars and one creamer?"

"Yeah."

Delight morphed into euphoria. He remembered? Biting her lower lip to control her smile, she took the mug and moved to sit next to the stove ... which just happened to be next to him. The small tent proved to be the best part of the expedition so far.

She took a sip of the coffee. The instant brew shouldn't taste like gourmet, but it did. She closed her eyes and savored the next sip.

Gunnar cleared his throat. When she glanced at him,

pink climbed up his neck as he fiddled with breakfast. Interesting. Why was he blushing? She grinned into her mug. Now they were even.

"Looks like banana-flavored buckwheat this morning." Gunnar read the instant breakfast packet, then poured hot water into it. "Wonder if it tastes like your banana bread?"

She'd gotten more words out of him in the last five minutes than all the days before. Heck, aside from his purge of words at the pool, he'd turned downright chatty. Which meant one of two things. Either he had nervous energy rushing through him like she did, or he was getting comfortable around her again.

Maybe both.

The only time she'd ever seen Gunnar Rebel nervous was when he'd finally made a move on her in high school. He'd been a complete mess, vacillating between tripping over his words and rushing them out so fast she hadn't been able to keep up with his train of thought. Then, as if he'd snapped, he'd grabbed hold of her arms and kissed her softly on the lips. It was one of her favorite memories. Well, almost all of her memories of Gunnar were her favorites.

What was stopping her from doing the snapping this time? If there was the possibility of something between them, why didn't she dive in and see? Sure, it might make things awkward between them, but they already were, weren't they?

She was tired of waiting, tired of running the trails solo. After everything that had happened to both of them, all the heartache and adversities they'd been through separately, she finally had the love of her life around her again. Staring at Gunnar as he prepared breakfast, she set her mug down. Her heart raced at full speed in her chest. If there was a chance at not having to do life alone anymore, she would grab it, all two hundred plus pounds of him, and hold on for dear life.

## 19

Gunnar forced himself to focus on stirring the pouch of buckwheat porridge. The atmosphere shifted, boomed thick with awareness, as Julie set her mug to the side. He chanced a peek at her, not able to resist discovering why the air had changed.

She'd set her jaw, and her fingers flexed into fists before she scooted closer. It wasn't a big move. Space to scoot was limited. Yet, with that one movement, she'd erased the distance between them.

Gunnar set the spoon down and leaned his shoulder a little toward her. Man, she was beautiful, even with her hair stuck up wildly from her braid and her eyes still puffy from sleep. The desire to wake up every morning to this blared loud in his mind.

"The coffee's perfect." Her voice, barely above a whisper, kicked his pulse to a gallop.

"Good." He took a deep breath, trying to calm his heart down.

Her gaze darted to his lips. They were so close that he watched in fascination as her eyes dilated.

Holy cow.

Was she really going to kiss him?

All hope of keeping his heart in check flew out the window. She leaned closer, millimeter by millimeter. He stayed where he was, not wanting to break the spell but also knowing he didn't have the right to make the first move. He did, however, shift his shoulder down and back so his body angled more toward her and he could watch her better.

She was so close her breath tickled his neck below his ear. They weren't touching, but the heat bouncing between them could catch the tent on fire. He swallowed, but all moisture had evaporated from his throat.

"Do you want peanut butter in it like you used to put in your oatmeal?" He barely recognized his voice and didn't give a hoot about food.

She smiled, a delicious, radiant smile that tempted him to close the centimeters between them and capture it. He'd buy her gallons of peanut butter if it kept that look on her face. He lifted his hand to cup her cheek and run his thumb across her lips but dropped it to his side before he touched her.

She moved closer, angling her head so their noses almost brushed. His pulse roared in his ears, begging him to close the distance. He'd dreamed of kissing her again for years, yearned to hold her close and never let go. Letting her take the lead tested all his self-control.

"Mmm, I love peanut butter." Her lips brushed his as she spoke, sending a shiver through him.

He'd never, not in a million years, thought this would

happen again. Her hand trailed up his arm, his muscles contracting like she'd pumped them full of electricity. If she didn't kiss him soon, he'd combust.

"Jules."

Her name tumbled out low, the tortured sound shouting his agony. She shifted, her body angling even closer. His breaths came in short bursts. He fought the need to close his eyes as she slightly touched the corner of his mouth. It wasn't a kiss, not really, but the feel of her smile against his skin rushed sparkling joy through his veins.

The zipper to the tent door ripped through the air, shattering the moment. Julie jumped away so fast, the cool air where she'd been jolted Gunnar. He growled as he glared at Sunny crawling in. She couldn't have waited another minute? Julie glanced at him, her cheeks flushed bright red, then hid her head as she took a drink of her coffee.

"I'm telling you, folks, temps on the Arctic sea ice are no joke." Sunny closed the door with one hand while holding a camera in the other.

She'd been filming all winter, driving Gunnar nuts with it. After her business partner had split with all their money and gear last spring, she'd taken time off from the climbing community. Mount Denali wasn't going anywhere, and she wanted adventure on her own. Her social media channel had exploded with each new video she posted about her solo adventures.

"Want to know how you can tell if it's cold or not?" Sunny leaned into the camera like she was going to tell a secret. "Boogers. That's how."

Julie snickered, the sounds cooling the frustration

firing through Gunnar. They'd always laughed and joked in the past, especially when Sunny had tagged along. His sister lived up to her name, bringing brightness to those around them.

"Take this lug, for instance." Sunny turned the camera on him.

"Sunny." He lifted an eyebrow in caution as he stirred peanut butter into Julie's breakfast.

"Yesterday was booger-freezing cold, like step outside and in two seconds your boogers are solid. We came up to these pressure ridges where the sea ice buckles up from the movement of the ocean."

"Coffee?" Gunnar interrupted her, hoping she'd stop her story.

She didn't—just kept right on talking over him. "When I stopped next to him, he had booger icicles hanging from his nose." Her words jumped out as she chuckled. "I wasn't sure if he'd turned into a walrus or what."

Julie burst out laughing, leaning against his side in her merriment. He shook his head and smiled. He'd take any embarrassment Sunny threw his way if it got Julie belly laughing.

"Let's eat and get going." He handed Julie her breakfast, then turned to make Sunny hers.

Julie bumped him with her shoulder. "Thanks."

She looked at him, a coy smile on her lips. Her gaze darted to his mouth before she tucked into her breakfast. His arms were light as new snow as he finished the meal and packed up. They'd be finishing what she'd started. He'd make sure of that.

JULIE STARED across the open lead of frigid sea water at Gunnar as he backstroked across the distance. When they'd reached the top of the pressure ridge and seen the expanse of water, they'd scanned up and down the sea ice shore with binoculars trying to locate where it connected again. With the ocean constantly moving, leads like this could open and shut, sometimes within hours. Yet, in the miles both ways they could view from that vantage, the ribbon of water stretched into the horizon. The only way forward would be to ferry everything and everyone across in the flat-bottomed canoe strapped to her sled, but first, someone had to stretch a rope to the other side of the water.

Gunnar had donned his water suit that fit over all his outerwear, leaving only his face exposed. The suit should keep him dry, theoretically. Yet, one catch on sharp ice, one tear through the fabric, and they'd be battling the clock against hypothermia. With her stuck on the opposite side of the lead with all their supplies, he might not make it.

Should they have waited for the others to catch up?

No.

She paced along the edge of the temporary shore. Their job today was to find a site for camp and get set up. If they didn't do their end of the work, then the others would suffer. She glanced behind her at the pressure ridge that practically shot straight out of the water they'd just spent the last hour crossing. Too bad the best place to set up camp was on the other side of the water.

Exhaustion pulled at her after the taxing climb over

the ridge. But when hadn't it since they took off for the Pole?

Well, she hadn't been all that tired that morning when she'd almost kissed Gunnar. Nope. Energy had flowed through her like she'd hooked up to a generator, only to have the kill switch pushed when Sunny interrupted.

The ice groaned beneath her feet, almost like it shared Julie's frustration. She shouldn't be trying to kiss Gunnar anyway. The Arctic Ocean that spent every minute of every day trying to kill them wasn't the place to rekindle the fire. They both needed to be on—one-thousand percent on. Yet, thinking about how close she'd come to kissing him had snuck into her thoughts throughout the day, dragging her attention from where it should be.

She gazed across the water. Gunnar just had a few more feet, and he'd be on solid ground again. Well, as solid as constantly shifting ice got.

"You're almost there." Julie cupped her hands around her mouth as she hollered.

He tipped his head back to look behind him, then rolled to his belly. He had to be freezing by now. While the suit kept him dry, it did nothing to fight the cold.

Julie held her breath as he reached his arms to the surface. He kicked, trying to hike himself up, but couldn't make it. Adjusting, he tried again, only to slip and fall back into the water.

She wanted to smash her eyes closed so she couldn't watch, but they were glued open. His arm swung to the ice again, but the motion looked sluggish. The cold would zap his energy if he didn't get out and warm up.

"Use your ax." She hoped he heard her over his struggling.

He brought the ax tied to his waist up and slammed it into the ice. When he tried to pull up, he couldn't get his upper body high enough to leverage himself out of the water. He flopped back into the water, leaning his side against the unrelenting edge.

"I can't get purchase with my feet." How could his voice be so calm?

She was freaking out and wasn't even the one in the water. Scanning the edge of the ice, she spotted a place that looked thicker than the other. Though, the terrain had a way of tricking one into thinking one thing, like that the ice stretched forever, only to pop open in a deep and wide crack. She hoped what she thought she saw was really there.

"Gunnar, try over that way." She pointed to the space that looked like it had more depth. "I think it's thicker there."

He swam over, his motions getting slower and slower. What if he couldn't get himself out? They'd tied a rope to him, but what if she couldn't drag him back fast enough? What if she couldn't lift him from the water?

"There! Right there," she yelled when he got to the spot, her voice frantic compared to his calm.

He leaned against the ice, his entire body heaving as he sucked in breaths. She prayed—begged that he could get out. She shook out her heavy arms like it would help him.

The ax swung with a speed she hadn't thought Gunnar had left. The thwack as it connected with the ice reached all the way across the lead to her. He pulled with both arms, but his hands slipped down the handle. Tears welled in her eyes, and she shook her head at the hopelessness welling in her.

His anguished roar let a tear free to slide down her cheek and fogged up her goggles. With the sound spurring him on, he lifted himself out of the water and flopped onto the ice. A sob broke from Julie as she fell to her knees. He'd made it.

He lifted his arm up in triumph, and Julie half laughed, half cried in relief. Didn't this just prove that letting her attraction to Gunnar distract her right now wasn't an option? If she'd been focused on terrain instead of daydreaming about what would've happened if Sunny hadn't come into the tent that morning, she could've seen that the ledge was more suited for climbing out off to the side.

She whipped her goggles off and dried her eyes. Keeping her head on straight mattered more than her relationship with Gunnar. One slip and someone could die. She couldn't let her distraction cause that. Besides, there would always be work to do or people around. She didn't want everyone to witness her and Gunnar acting like a couple of love-struck teenagers.

"You okay?" She needed to get back to task, and that meant getting him moving again.

"Yeah." He groaned as he rolled over to his side and pushed himself up.

"Get moving then." Turning to the sled to follow her own advice, she double-checked ties connecting the sled to the raft.

When he got his wind back, he'd be pulling her over on the raft with the supplies. They had at least six trips across the lead and back to get the sleds and dogs to the other side. Her arms hurt just thinking about all the pulling ahead of her.

Then, they had camp to set up at the spot half a mile off of the lead Gunnar had scoped out through the binoculars and needed to be ready to help the others when they finally arrived. The day still had too much work to be done. Daydreaming about kissing and what ifs wasn't an option.

## 20

---

J ulie tugged on the clunky sled stuck on yet another pressure ridge, her muscles aching from the long, grueling hours. While her sled was lighter than the ones the other team members handled, the extra length that the rafts strapped to the bottom added made some ridges exponentially difficult to navigate. The last five days since that first night on the ice, the towering obstacles had plagued the expedition. Traversing the boulder-sized blocks of ice and snow all tumbled together like a forgotten pile of children's building blocks not only exhausted them all, dogs included, but it slowed them down.

The first few days, the team had approached each ridge with gusto. Now, though, tensions soared. With the travel slowed to a crawl, the race to the North Pole was more of a plod.

The only upside of the long, hard days was the collapse into the tent at night. She and the Rebels had settled into an easy camaraderie, joking through dinner before they all fell into their sleeping bags, practically snoring before their heads hit the pillows. On the nights Sunny didn't get the coveted middle spot, Julie found herself pressed against Gunnar's side. Sure, layers and layers of fabric separated them, but his solid presence and warmth filled her with a jubilation she hadn't had since high school.

She glanced down at where Gunnar and Mason waited for her, then gave the sled another yank. Working with the team solidified her earlier revelation that she didn't want to be so alone anymore. Having others to lean on, even when their attitudes turned grumpy, made her realize just how empty she'd let her emotional tank get. After her father's death the year before, she'd just kind of tucked her head to the wind and plunged forward. Maybe if she had lifted her head and searched the horizon for others eager to come alongside her, she wouldn't have ended up bent low to the ground with the weight of loneliness upon her.

When they arrived at the checkpoint later that evening—if they made it—she owed Saylor a big hug. Her cousin had tried to get through to Julie. She'd just been too stubborn and unwilling to burden anyone with her emotions. Maybe the time had come for her to sell the place she and her father had built in the wilderness between Valdez and Glenallen and relocate to a more populated area.

The sled lurched as it broke from the ice wall it had wedged against. Julie stumbled, her feet slipping on the loose snow. Catching herself on an ice boulder beside her, she huffed out a breath to steady her shaking hands. She needed to stay focused. There wouldn't be a future to contemplate if she tumbled down this ridge and died.

"You okay?" Gunnar hollered from the bottom where he paced, ready to jump into action if needed.

She waved, then picked her next step down the jumbled mess.

"Okay, boys, let's get this sled down. I'm ready to get to the checkpoint." She talked to the four dogs hooked to the sled to help her. "Easy now. Hup."

The dogs pulled on the leads, dragging the sled on the path between the ice. Having her entire team hooked up on these ridges just caused tangles and fights. Keeping to her two leads and the wheel dogs meant she had enough brute force to move the sled easily, without the others getting in the way. The arrangement worked but meant more time hooking and unhooking her team on each ridge she came to.

The sled slammed into another low wall of ice and jerked the dogs to a halt. She wanted to cry. Just throw herself over the sled and have a good wail. Exhaustion would do that to a person. Since it wouldn't do a lick of good, she climbed over the front of the sled to see what it was hung up on.

"Let's go!" Mason yelled up, his frustration not helping the situation any.

Angry words bubbled up like a bottle of soda shook hard. They wouldn't do anything but add more tension, so she swallowed them down. Gunnar crossed his arms and glared at Mason. Mason threw up his hands in apology and stomped off to his sled. Julie got his impatience. Sunny and Clark had gone ahead to scout, so Mason was stuck here waiting on Julie.

Waiting sucked in the Arctic. It gave the cold time to
seep into the layers of clothes as the body stopped
producing heat with the inactivity. From the way Mason
marched around his sled, his arms swinging and legs
lifted high, this latest stall in progress froze him. Yet, here
she was, unzipping her coat another inch to keep herself
from sweating with exertion.

"Want help?" Gunnar called up.

"No, I can get it" She signaled him to stay put.

By the time he climbed the hill, she'd probably have
the stupid sled unstuck. The front corner wedged against
a block of ice the size of a large pumpkin. It shouldn't be
too hard to push free. Placing her feet on the sled, she
squeezed her body between the ice and gear to get more
leverage. She pressed hard on the runners, groaning with
the strain against her already tired muscles.

"Hup! Hup!" Her command to the dogs faltered from
her mouth as the sled jolted free and careened over the
ice too fast for her to control.

A shrill scream from the dogs had black spots dancing
before Julie's eyes. She leaped for the sled as it raced past
her. Frantic yipping curdled fear in her belly. Snagging the
back of the sled, she pulled with all her might. Her mittens
couldn't wrap around the material, and the sled slipped in
her grip. She ripped her mittens off with her teeth so she
only wore her glove liners and caught it in a tighter hold.

Each inch the sled slipped, her dogs' yips of pain
spiked to cries of agony. She braced her feet on the ice the
sled had been stuck on, praying that her muscles
wouldn't give out. The sled's nose tipped lower, yanking
at her muscles.

"No." She roared at the searing pain in her arms and the betrayal of the stupid sled suddenly eager to get off the ridge.

She couldn't. Her fingers were slipping. Her guttural growl filled her ears as she put all her strength into leaning back. Muscles shaking, the sled edged backward. Just a little more and the dogs could get free.

Her feet slipped off their perch, crashing her to the ground and knocking the air out of her. She scrambled to grab the sled as terrified screams filled the air. Tears blurred her vision. She'd killed her dogs.

The sled jerked to a stop.

Julie blinked in confusion.

"Hurry, Jules." Gunnar's strained voice shook her into action.

She scrambled over the ice wall the sled had been squeezing through. The sled pinned her father's favorite dog, Pax's, back end to the ground. He whined and scratched his front paws at the snow, trying to get away. Mason stumbled up the ice and leaned his shoulder on the opposite side of the sled from Gunnar just as Julie crawled between their legs to the dog.

"Okay. We lift on three. Jules, slide Pax away." Veins popped out of Gunnar's forehead with the strain of holding the sled still.

"Wait. Let me unhook him." She cut the neckline and tugline from the harness, then worked her arms around Pax's trembling body. "Okay."

"Three, two, one." Gunnar groaned as he lifted the sled.

She eased the dog from under the sled. Bright red

blood trailed on the snow, but she refused to let it distract her. Pax jerked his legs, trying to get free.

"Easy now, big boy." She crooned to him as she lifted his bulk into her arms. Her knees almost buckled with the weight. "Let's get you off this heap and see what's going on."

She carefully picked her way off of the pressure ridge. Gunnar's commands to the rest of her dogs floated down from behind her, but she kept her focus on reaching the bottom without dropping Pax. Her foot slipped and her knee rammed into the sharp edge of an ice chunk.

"You okay?" Gunnar called from behind.

"Fine." She gritted her teeth and pushed to her feet.

Just a few more feet, and she'd be there. When she reached flat ice, she carried Pax to Gunnar's sled and placed him carefully on the snow. She peeked at the men almost down off the ridge, then turned all her attention on the dog.

Blood soaked the fur on his back leg. Pulling her glove liners off, she ignored the bite of the frigid air against her bare skin as she pushed aside the fur to examine the injury. Pax whined and lifted his head to look at her.

"I know, boy. I'm sorry." She choked on the words and blinked away the tears.

The more she wiped at the blood, the more saturated the fur became. Crimson dripped and pooled beneath the dog. Her lunch rushed up her throat, but she swallowed it down.

Gunnar ran up to his sled and unloaded supplies onto the ice. His calm, smooth movements eased her nerves a small fraction. He would know what to do.

He pulled the first-aid kit off the sled and rushed to her side. "Status?"

"His leg. It's bleeding too much to see what's wrong." Julie shifted to the other side of the dog to let Gunnar have better access.

"Anything else?" Gunnar fired the question without looking up from examining the wound.

"I don't know." She hadn't even checked.

"No worries. Biggest injury to littlest." He wiped away the blood with gauze, shaking his head.

A deep gash the length of her hand ran from the top of Pax's leg down. Gunnar prodded the wound, making Pax whine.

"I know, boy. It's gonna be okay." Julie petted his head as she braced him from moving.

"The cut hasn't exposed bone, thank God, but it's big." Gunnar dug through his first-aid kit. "I can't flush it out without the water freezing."

"Will he be okay?" Her fingers trembled in the dog's fur.

Gunnar sighed with a shrug.

"Do we need to put him down?" Mason tossed Julie her mittens she'd abandoned, his words sending sharp shards of cold up her arms.

"Mason," Gunnar rumbled a low warning.

"I'm sorry." Mason crouched down next to her. "Julie, you know I'm sorry, but we talked about this."

They had. The possibility of injury and death was high out here, not only for the dogs, but for them as well. It wouldn't be right to keep a dog in misery if a severe injury happened, especially with help so far away. She stared at Gunnar, praying he said no, but preparing herself for the worst.

"The checkpoint is close." He tore open a QuikClot gauze and positioned it on the gash. "Let's get him to the vet."

Julie nodded, relief stinging her eyes. It didn't mean Pax was out of the woods. She still might have to make the call to put him down. But with the vet so close, she could hold off on that decision.

"Mason, go hook up Julie's team." Gunnar yanked another QuikClot out of the first-aid kit. "We need to move, ASAP."

Mason squeezed her shoulder, pulling her in for a hurried side hug, then took off for her team.

"Jules, get the roll of gauze and tape." Gunnar snapped the order.

She reached over the dog and pulled the gauze from the medical bag. Her fingers shook violently, making it hard to open the package. Gunnar wrapped his hand around hers.

"He's"—Julie choked on her words—"he's Dad's favorite."

"I know, honey. I know." Gunnar tightened his hold on her hands. "One step at a time."

"Okay."

"Together. We get through this together."

She nodded, any answer she could give clogging in her throat. Whatever happened when they got to the checkpoint, she wouldn't have to do it alone. Gunnar was here, and, at least for now, she could trust his promise to always be there when she needed.

## 21

G unnar finished spooning the last of the dog food soup into the dog bowl and turned to the series of interconnected, long, half-tubed tents used for the checkpoints. He'd seen similar used in Antarctica, regions of the Himalayas, and at pop-up military bases, but Mason had gone all out with the ridiculous length.

Why would they need a structure that large for a one-night stay? It had to be a pain to breakdown and construct at each checkpoint the farther the expedition team got to the North Pole. Waste of time and money, but then again, it wasn't Gunnar's dollar.

He pushed the door open for the first time since they'd arrived and froze at the chaos before him. A field of reporters huddled in groups of two and three, chattering like an unkindness of ravens. The phrase that so perfectly fit the birds, also fit the people.

Tucking his head to avoid being recognized, Gunnar weaved through the press area to a section of the tent lined with computers. Saylor leaned over the shoulder of a person at a computer, examining the screen. The scowl on her face said whatever she saw there wasn't good news.

"Where's Julie?" He stepped up to Saylor while he scanned the rest of the room.

"Things are good here. Thanks for asking." Saylor glared at the screen, not looking at Gunnar.

"Sorry." Gunnar lifted his hands in surrender.

Being friendly with the fire-breathing dragon guarding the princess might go a long way toward his happy ending. His lips twitched at the image that flitted through his head of Saylor billowing smoke. He'd do whatever he could to show Saylor he didn't mean Julie any harm, that a life together like it always should have been was his goal now.

Seeing Julie at the top of the pressure ridge, struggling on her own, solidified his purpose in his core. He didn't want another day to pass without her in it. Didn't want to summit life's struggles without her hand in his.

"Let me know if that weather system shifts." Saylor patted the desk jockey on the shoulder and faced Gunnar, crossing her arms over her chest. "What happened out there?"

"Sea ice happened." He closed his eyes and gritted his teeth until he could rein in his frustration. "Look, I know you don't like me. I don't like myself too much, either." He huffed and unzipped his coat as Saylor's expression softened, and she dropped her arms. "It's been a long, horrible day, and I just want to make sure Julie's okay."

Saylor glanced at the door in the back of the room separating the computers from the rest of the temporary building. Her hands flexed into fists as her jaw shifted in thought. He didn't need her directions. It wouldn't take much to find Julie, but if he wanted a relationship with her to last, he needed to make peace with her cousin.

Saylor nodded as she came to some kind of internal decision, then stepped right up into Gunnar's space. Fire burned him from her glare, but he caught a hint of worry there as well. She poked him in the chest ... hard.

"I don't know what your end game is, Rebel, but if you hurt her again, I will hunt you down, drug you, tie your arms to your dog team, and have them pull until your limbs rip from your body. Then I'll boil them up and serve them to your dogs. Capeesh?" Without a doubt, Saylor would follow through with the threat.

"Got it." Gunnar swallowed.

She was scarier than a lot of the men he'd seen in the military.

"Good. Follow the tent to the end. That's where the vet is." Saylor pointed to the door, then stomped past Gunnar, yelling as she left. "Ron, we need to make sure we restock the sleds."

Gunnar took a deep breath, glad the gatekeeper had left, then made his way to the door. Katie Cullens talked with a helper at another desk, her recorder shoved so close to the man he could lick it. Gunnar tucked his chin down and tried to make himself blend in. He'd almost made it past Katie when she glanced up. Her eyes widened, and a satisfied smirk graced her lips.

"Lieutenant Rebel, a word, please." She shoved her recorder in front of Gunnar.

"Busy." He went to step past, but she shifted, just like she had in Utqiagvik.

If any reporter fit the name of a group of ravens, she did. Unkind. Calculating. He could see her spinning a tale from bits of half-truths, looking at how she could angle a story to her benefit.

"Whose carelessness caused the dog's injury? Do you think the animal will survive or has another musher sacrificed an innocent being for their own glory?" The rise of her eyebrow and thoughtless words ignited Gunnar's already short fuse.

He stepped closer, crowding her space and using his height to his advantage. "Every single one of us loves our dogs. We'd rather be injured than them, but accidents happen. Your heartless questions prove you don't get it. Don't get Alaskans."

The hard, calculating mask fell as she moved back a step. Eyes darting anywhere but at him, her chin trembled, and he almost felt sorry for pushing. She squared her shoulders and turned her gaze back on him, her remorse short-lived.

Gunnar shook his head as he scanned the room. Mason and Clark huddled in a corner. Clark leaned in close to Mason, his cheeks red as he whispered to his best friend. Mason shook his head and crossed his arms. Gunnar should probably see what was going on with them, but Julie came first.

"Lieutenant Rebel, what about the fact that the expedition isn't going as planned? Your team should've arrived at this latitude two days ago." Katie's question forced his attention back to her. Though her voice had recovered its strength, one arm crossed over her stomach like she held herself strong.

"If you have questions, ask Mason." Gunnar pointed to the corner where Mason and Clark still argued.

Her arm dropped from her stomach and eyes narrowed. Gunnar may have just sent a cunning raven to his friends to peck for answers, but he didn't care. Julie needed him, and he wasn't about to let her down again.

## 22

Julie sat in a chair pulled up to the folding table, rubbing her hand over Pax's head. The sedative had him sleeping, but every once in a while, he'd whine, his leg twitching. She stared at his black mask that faded to tan, wishing she could see his bright blue eyes.

As she buried her face against his warm fur, a tear tracked a cold path down her cheek. What was she even doing here? Mushing had always been what drove life, first in her father's career, then in hers, but the stress of racing, of making sponsors happy, suffocated her. How had her father dealt with it?

Pax groaned, and Julie massaged between his shoulders. Because of her drive to be the best, to follow her father's trail, Pax would never run again. He'd never join his team and rush down the trails he loved with his tongue hanging out his mouth.

Why was she even doing this expedition?

She'd lost her father, her childhood, what pathetic

life she had to this sport. Couldn't she find a better way to merge her love of mushing with making a living? Heck, maybe it was time to find a job not tangled up with dogs and a sport that required everything from her.

She shook her head and sat up with a sniff. Could she really even consider giving up on racing? While the stress did knot in her stomach, she loved the thrill of running the trails and competing against the best in the world. But was that thrill enough?

"What do you want, Jules?" She groaned and scanned the small room set up as a field surgery.

Exhaustion weighed on her mind, making it slow and dramatic. She should just rest. Maybe then her brain wouldn't circle with doubts. Thoughts she shouldn't let freeze solid during an expedition that demanded her all. The future was best left alone until after they reached the North Pole.

She didn't really know what she wanted, anyway.

The door swung open and in stomped Gunnar.

Scratch that.

She knew exactly what she wanted.

Even as messed up as their past was and as much as she feared he'd break her heart again, she wanted to find out if life had more for them together. Doing so may leave her broken-hearted again, but hadn't she spent the last fifteen years like that already?

His attention stayed glued on her, assessing her as he crossed the room. She was out of the chair and into his arms before he made it halfway to her. Tears she'd bottled up streamed from her eyes in an embarrassing rush.

Gunnar said nothing, not that it surprised her. Didn't

shush her like her father always had or say everything would be okay.

Nope.

Gunnar just wrapped his arms firmly around her, leaning his head against hers. His quiet comfort multiplied her yearning for him, for the acceptance and respect he always gave to her.

She tucked her face into his neck and breathed in the crisp air that still clung to his skin. The burdens of Pax's injury—shoot, of what to do with the kennel as a whole—lifted with his steady support. Not that she needed him to make the decision of what to do. Not at all. But having him there with her, knowing she could ask him for suggestions and he wouldn't give a knee-jerk answer, gave her a confidence she didn't have on her own.

With one arm secured around her waist, he rubbed the other hand up her spine. Her tension snapped like cracking sea ice warmed by the sun. If he kept it up, she'd float away. She closed her eyes, took a deep breath, and blew it out slowly.

"Better?" His low question rumbled in her ear, melting more of her tension away.

"Yeah."

"How's Pax?"

And that was why she loved Gunnar. Three words. With three words, he'd shown what was important: her and the dog.

She peeked up at him. The concern etched on his face as he took in Pax lying on the exam table rushed the rest of her stress and doubt away. No matter what her mushing future held, she'd make sure, come flood waters or freeze, that Gunnar Rebel ran the trails ahead with her.

She kissed him on the cheek, his beard tickling her skin, then moved back to the table to continue her vigil over the dog. "He's stable. The vet won't know until she gets him back to Fairbanks if he'll lose the leg or not."

Gunnar pulled a chair next to hers and combed his fingers through Pax's fur. She pressed her leg against Gunnar's and rubbed Pax's ear like she knew he liked. The peacefulness of the moment quieted her racing thoughts.

"I'm glad you're here." She ran her hand down the dog's neck, bumping up against Gunnar's.

He captured her fingers with his and brought them to his lips. The tender kiss tingled up her arm. After placing her hand back on Pax's side, Gunnar dragged her chair right up next to his, draped his arm over the back of the seat, then went back to petting the dog.

"I'm not going anywhere." He ran his palm over her skin as he stroked Pax's fur. "Never again."

The tingles from Gunnar's touch oozed into a warm puddle of happiness in her belly. She folded her feet beneath her and leaned against him. His arm wrapped around her back, anchoring her to him. As promises went, him always staying with her was one she hoped he would keep.

## 23

The wind gusted hard against the side of the tent, popping loud in Julie's ears. She cringed and rubbed the pain the noise caused away. The last three days, the wind had mostly kept a constant stream, causing a thwacking sound as the tent flexed on its supports. Just enough wind to blow the snow around and make it impossible to see, but not enough to cause any real problems.

Annoying?

Yes.

Disheartening?

A little.

Being stuck in the tent, not able to make any leeway to the Pole, pinched. Yet, they all knew the weather could make or break the expedition. She just wished they had stayed at the checkpoint like Clark had argued for, instead of leaving when they knew a storm front was headed their way. They hadn't made it a full day's mush away before the swirling snow had forced them to stop.

Another good gust punched the tent. Julie flinched, then jumped when the zipper opened. A flurry of snow whipped into the tent, slicing through her wool sweater. The propane stove flickered, threatening to extinguish. She blocked the wind the best she could to keep it from going out as the Rebels climbed in.

"How are the dogs?" she asked Gunnar as soon as he had the door zipped tight.

"Great. Curled up, sleeping." He shrugged out of his parka, and Julie had to pull her eyes away from the stretch of his broad shoulders against the fabric of his shirt.

The worst part about being stuck in a whiteout in a tiny tent was not being able to get Gunnar alone. If they'd stayed at the checkpoint, not only could they move around, but she could've found somewhere to drag the tempting wall of muscle to and see if his kisses still turned her knees to liquid goo.

Since they had to stop for the weather, the only time she could have him to herself was when they'd go to check on the dogs. Call her crazy but taking the time to kiss when the snow whipped against her face like little shards of glass wasn't her idea of romantic. The closest she got to any sign of intimacy was when it was her turn to sleep in the middle, and Gunnar would lie close and rest his hand on her hip.

Even through the layers of clothing and sleeping bags, the weight of his palm would burn her side, long into the next day. She wished he'd just pull her close and wrap his arms around her fully. With Sunny in the tent, Julie understood why he didn't. Still, she yearned to snuggle into his embrace.

"How are the boys?" She scooted away from the stove so Sunny could have the heat to warm up.

"Better." Sunny chuckled. "Clark's finally forgiven Mason for not listening to him."

Julie smirked and shook her head. In the four months she'd trained with them, she'd never seen them argue. Good thing they weren't fighting anymore. Being stuck in a tent and not getting along would be torture.

"Mason talked to Saylor." Gunnar plopped down close to Julie, rubbing his hand across her shoulders. "Pax is doing good. He's been moving his leg more, so the vet's hopeful there isn't anything broken."

Julie leaned her head against Gunnar's shoulder with a sigh. She'd worried about her dog almost constantly. The weather had made it impossible for the vet to fly out with Pax. Hearing that his leg had improved coursed relief through her. There still was a chance he could lose the leg, or worse, but she'd take any good news she could get.

"It also looks like the storm should blow through tomorrow afternoon at the latest." Sunny pulled a book out of her pack as she settled in.

"That's a new one." Julie motioned to the book.

Sunny had brought a couple with her, swapping out for new ones at the checkpoints. All of them had been romance. Julie never read that genre. Frankly, after Gunnar had left, reading about characters' happily-ever-afters depressed her.

When she did read, she stuck to epic fantasy. She loved the sweeping worlds and journeys to fight against evil and triumph. Plus, anything with a dragon got her excited.

"Bristol North is one of my favorite authors." Sunny stretched the book to Julie. "She writes these funny romantic suspenses set in Alaska. You'd love them."

Julie turned the book over in her hand and skimmed the back cover. Maybe now that Gunnar was back in her life, adding a romance into her to-be-read list every now and then wouldn't wrench at her heart. There were even a ton of fantasy romances she could dive into that she'd avoided like the plague.

"Bristol is from Alaska, but I haven't been able to figure out where. I'm thinking she's writing under a pen name." Sunny wrapped her hair into a messy bun and took the book back.

Gunnar's low chuckle settled warmth in Julie's gut like she'd just taken a shot of seal oil. How could the rumbling sound affect her like that? Maybe because he'd been doing it more and more the farther north they went.

Sunny's gaze zeroed in on Gunnar. "You know something. I can tell."

"I know where she lives." Gunnar pulled his deck of cards out and tapped the box against his hand.

"Really?" Sunny lit up like a kid at Christmas.

Man, she must really like this author.

"Yep." Gunnar shuffled his cards, then looked at Julie. "Poker or rummy?"

She pressed her lips together to contain her smile as Sunny huffed.

"Well ... tell me who she is?" Sunny shook the book in Gunnar's direction.

"Nope." Gunnar popped the "p" for emphasis.

Sunny glared across the tent at him, but he just ignored her and dealt the cards. Julie's gaze bounced between the two, loving the sibling back and forth that she'd missed so much. When he didn't answer, Sunny lifted her eyebrow in a look that meant war.

"Did Gunnar tell you he read quite a few books over the winter?" Sunny smiled a calculated look at Julie.

"Um ... no." She tried to stifle her amusement.

"Sunniva." Gunnar never used Sunny's full name.

Whatever she had on him must be good.

"He practically devoured my romances. He'd snatch them up before I could even get to them." Sunny played up the drama.

"Not true." Gunnar tossed a card into Julie's growing pile. "And you'll never find out about Bristol now."

"So, you didn't read the books?" Julie grabbed up her cards but didn't look at them.

He stared at his hand, his mouth shifting to the side in thought as he moved cards around. "No, I read them."

"Okay." Julie snickered and glanced at Sunny, who rolled her eyes.

"I just didn't devour them like my twerp of a sister is claiming."

"What did you think?"

"They were ..." His pause had Julie leaning closer. "Enlightening."

He speared her with a look so steeped with heat she wondered just what was in these books of Sunny's. His eyes dropped to Julie's cracked lips that were far from attractive. Yet, the longer he stared at them, the more she wanted to lean over, chapped lips or not, and press them to his. He winked at her, and instantly her cheeks were on fire.

"Ugh, stop." Sunny whacked Gunnar on the arm with

the book. "I only read clean romance, and you know it, you lug."

"Sure." He drew out the word.

"Really. Anything more than kissing, and I get uncomfortable." Now, Sunny's cheeks bloomed a bright red. "That's not to say the scenes aren't steamy."

"You've got that right." Gunnar wagged his eyebrows up and down, earning another whack from the book.

"They just don't go too far," Sunny continued, throwing another glare at Gunnar before softening it. "Please, you have to tell me who Bristol North is."

"Don't think so." Gunnar lifted his cards at Julie. "We playing?"

"Please." Sunny laid her hand on Gunnar's arm.

"It's a secret pen name for a reason, Sunny." He shrugged her hand off.

"I won't tell a soul. I promise." She replaced her hand. "You can trust me."

Gunnar stared at her, his face softening. "I know I can."

Since the expedition got on the way, Julie got the distinct impression that Sunny had a major issue with trust. Gunnar's soft words brought tears to Julie's eyes. He had to know how important it was to Sunny that he trust her.

"Okay, listen. I really can't tell you who she is, but what if I ask her to contact you?"

Julie liked that Gunnar wouldn't tell them the secret.

Sunny nodded, her excited look deflating a little. "I can respect that you don't want to break her trust. How'd you find out who she is?"

He shrugged, shifting the cards in his hands. "She

needed help moving some stuff. Some boxes tipped over and dumped a ton of her books." Gunnar stretched out his leg behind Julie, so it pushed along her body. "Are we playing or not?"

Julie tucked her head to her cards, pressing her lips tightly to contain her smile. Gunnar may not say a lot, but she was learning so much from the things that he did. One thing was for sure, he still wanted to see those he loved happy. It was what she'd always admired about him.

## 24

Gunnar pounded the last of the stakes into the ice to secure the dogs to. The last week had been like living through the movie *Groundhog Day*. Wake up, take care of dogs, break camp, mush through scenery of constant white and variations of blue, make camp, feed dogs, sleep, and repeat. If it wasn't for the evenings in the tent with Julie and Sunny, and the exhaustion, he'd likely go crazy. He guessed there was a lot to say for the monotony. It meant there had been no more emergencies.

The worst part was that there was never any time to get Julie alone. It wasn't like he and Julie could make out with his sister in the tent, and it just hadn't seemed like the right time when Julie was so upset about her dog. Gunnar snorted. This entire expedition was the worst time for a relationship. The best thing he could do was drop it until they got back to solid ground. Getting his mind to agree to that hadn't happened yet.

The dogs paced on their lines. By the end of the day,

they were normally ready to have dinner, bed down, and call it a night. Sure, they got excited when the soup pot came around, but they never acted up much while still hooked to the sled.

His lead dog, Rocky, whined and jumped over his partner, Bullwinkle. Farther down the line, Sylvester snarled at Minnie, who laid her ears back in return. Before Gunnar could get to them, they lunged for each other in a chaotic bid for it. Gunnar hollered and dashed to them, groaning in frustration and exhaustion when they finally calmed down.

They'd tangled themselves up on the line. Ripping off his mittens and stuffing them in his pocket, he grabbed one dog by the harness, unhooked her, and led her to her spot for the night. The cold froze his fingers as he snapped the clip onto her harness. If he could just get them unhooked from the sled, he could feed them, then untangle the line in the tent.

Julie's scream ripped through the air, freezing his clammy skin. He rushed past the dogs toward the tent, his heart pounding in his throat. Had the tent caught on fire? He couldn't see any smoke.

He skidded to a stop as the opening to the tent came into view. A polar bear had Julie's foot in its mouth and was dragging her out of the tent.

"Hey!" he yelled, picking up a crate of supplies at his feet and tossing it at the bear.

The box hit the bear in the flank. It flinched, dropped Julie, and turned to Gunnar. Lunging for the sled, Gunnar grabbed the shotgun from the supplies. The bear charged, and Gunnar pumped a shell into the chamber, lifted the gun, and pulled the trigger. Click. Nothing.

The bear barreled down on Gunnar. The dogs barked chaotically behind him. Julie yelled from where she stumbled to her feet by the tent. He didn't want to end up bear bait. Gunnar was out of options.

He braced his feet wide on the ice, flipped the shotgun in his hand, and swung with all his strength. The butt of the gun connected with the polar bear's head with a loud crack. The bear tripped sideways, its front legs giving out. Gunnar had little time before the stunned bear shook it off. He prayed it would just run away, but he couldn't count on that.

Quickly scanning the area for a weapon, he snatched the ax from the sled and backed away from the tent and dogs. If nothing else, he'd lead the predator away from everyone. The bear shook its head, focused its black glare on Gunnar, and huffed a threatening sound that made Gunnar brace for another charge.

Steam billowed from the bear's nostrils as it stomped its front foot, throwing snow out behind it. The ax handle bit into his skin that burned from the cold, but he gripped it tighter, ignoring the pain. The bear's muscles bunched, and everything else disappeared as Gunnar waited for it to lunge.

It charged, striding two steps before a boom shattered Gunnar's focus and echoed across the ice. The bear deterrent bullet sparkled like firecrackers at the bear's feet, then fizzled out. The bear flinched, roared a sound that liquified Gunnar's bones, and charged again.

Gunnar stumbled backward, adjusting his sweaty grip on the ax. Three quick shots exploded into the air, slamming into the bear's chest. It fell and huffed two labored breaths before it didn't move again.

Gunnar's knees gave out, and he collapsed onto the snow. He scanned the area to make sure the bear didn't have a buddy, his survey stopping on Julie and Sunny. Julie held a smoking shotgun still trained on the animal as she made her way to Gunnar. Sunny shoved the bear deterrent launcher into her pocket with a huff and stomped over to the dogs.

Julie's limp drew Gunnar's attention. "You're hurt."

"It's nothing." She knelt in the snow next to him, her chest heaving as her gaze darted over him. "I thought he was going to get you."

She leaned forward, resting her face against his neck, and he wrapped her in a hug. He'd almost lost her. He tightened his hold on her.

"When Sunny shot that sparkler, and it didn't leave" —Julie pulled back, her head shaking as she turned to look at the bear—"I had to shoot it."

"That bear was out to eat us." Gunnar's fingers burned from the cold when he flexed them, and he snatched his mittens from his pocket and stood. Mason, Clark, and Sunny all hurried to him and Julie. "We'll have to move camp. Go another mile or so away just in case the kill draws more bears."

Which meant it'd be dark by the time they got to a new location.

Mason whistled low, walking around the bear. "We heard the commotion, but by the time we got out of the tent, you all had finished with the excitement."

"We need to break camp and get going." Sunny stared at the sun low on the horizon. "No use standing around gawking."

She gave Gunnar a quick side hug, then rushed to the tent.

"Man, my stomach is rubbing my backbone." Clark rubbed his coat. "Guess dinner will have to wait."

"Here." Julie took an energy snack called a packaroon from where she always stashed a few inside her coat.

He caught it in the air with a toothy smile. "Thanks, Mom."

Julie smiled and rolled her eyes. It was a silly joke, but it got Gunnar thinking. Julie would be an amazing mom. She would push her kids to find adventures, but also be there with them, with homemade donuts and tons of love. Could they have that together? Did he deserve to even think about it when he'd so carelessly thrown his last chance at it away?

## 25

Julie extended her foot to the stove, wiggling her toes to increase circulation. The duct tape she'd wrapped around her boot to hold it together after the bear attack hadn't held. No surprise there, with how cold it was. Nothing worked well at forty below. Even though the few miles they mushed away from the bear hadn't taken more than an hour, the cold had seeped into her boot and frozen her toes. She just hoped the white color of her little digits wasn't frostbite setting in.

Her skin burned as it warmed, and she blew out a frustrated breath. There wasn't anything she could do for it but wait. She leaned toward the food supply and set up the dinner pouches for hot water. They'd just plumped up and were ready to eat when Gunnar and Sunny climbed into the tent.

"Dinner smells good." Gunnar's rumbled compliment pooled warmth in her stomach.

Downright silly. It wasn't like she'd slaved over the

stove or anything. Hot water in a pouch of freeze-dried food didn't equate cooking.

Julie's sudden obsession with homemaking was all Clark's fault with his mom comments. Well, that and the fact that the man she wanted to make a home with smashed himself close to her every night to keep her warm. It wasn't like it used to be, with him pulling her and her sleeping bag into his. Shoot, he didn't even wrap his arms around her or anything. But the press of his body against hers had all kinds of thoughts of family and future twirling in her mind.

Only to tailspin and crash when reality set in.

She couldn't have kids. Couldn't be a mom, like Clark joked. Cancer had stripped that from her when it had taken all her reproductive bits and pieces. Over the years, she'd accepted her fate. Yet, being here with Gunnar and there being a possibility of a future had doubt cawing in her mind like a bunch of ravens.

What would he think when he found out she couldn't have kids? He had to be ready for a family now that he was out of the military. Would the desire she caught in his eye when he looked at her dim when he knew the truth?

She squared her shoulders. If it changed his love for her, then he wasn't the right man for her. It would suck, but they both deserved the future they wanted, even if it wasn't together.

Gunnar plopped beside her and reached for her boot. He scowled as he examined the gaping hole and ripped duct tape. Setting it down, he shifted his position and grabbed her foot.

"We'll have to fix your boot." His hand cupped her heel, and he gently moved the toes around.

"Yeah. I have a spare, but they aren't as warm." Her leg jerked at his tickling touch.

"Hold still." He glared at her. "I think you might have frostbite."

"A little hard to hold still when you're tickling me." She twitched again, her exasperation shifting to a giggle.

"Interesting." He lifted her foot closer to his eyes, his expression shutting down her laughter.

Would she lose a toe?

"What?" Her question was barely more than a whisper.

"You're still ticklish." His devilish smile was the only warning she got before his fingers raced over the bottom of her foot.

She shrieked and tried to yank her foot away. He held on tight, never letting up on his assault. His low chuckle bubbled happiness from her. He could torture her for days if it meant she could hear that sound.

"Geesh. Knock it off, you two." Sunny swatted her brother, then reached for a dinner pouch. "You're worse than a couple of kids." She sounded grumpy, but her smile gave her away.

Gunnar stopped tickling. He pressed his fingers into Julie's feet in a massaging motion. Had she ever felt anything as relaxing or intimate before? Not since before he'd left. She opened her eyes that she had closed in bliss and found him staring at her, a satisfied smile hitching that one side of his mouth up.

Determination exploded in her chest. When she got

him alone, she was kissing the living daylights out of him. She'd deal with the doubts later. Having people constantly around both in the camp and at the checkpoints made finding privacy hard. The only time they'd been alone was when they sat with Pax, and she had been so overwhelmed with what would happen to her dog, she hadn't had one thought of taking advantage of the moment. Since then, opportunities for kissing were nil.

"That bear was something else." Sunny blew on her chowder, jolting Julie back to the present.

"Yeah." Gunnar gave Julie's foot a squeeze and set it near the stove. "Keep it there for a while. I don't want that spot getting worse."

She nodded and handed him his dinner. "Definitely don't want to lose a toe."

"Might lessen your chances with the fellas?" Sunny wagged her eyebrows and took a big bite.

"Nah. With winter nine months out of the year and mosquito season the other three, a fella wouldn't know until I already hooked and reeled him in." Julie poked her spoon at her dinner, keeping her gaze off Gunnar.

He growled low, eliciting a snort and a giggle from Sunny.

"You're right, Jules." Sunny played along. "The poor soul wouldn't know until your wedding day."

"I couldn't care less about how many toes you have or don't have." Gunnar stabbed his spoon at his dinner. "You've already got me on your line, no use casting for another."

Julie's cheeks hurt from her smile as Sunny gave Gunnar a hard time. When he finally peeked up at Julie, the vulnerability in his eyes did her in. She leaned in, not caring that Sunny watched with rapt attention.

Julie kissed him on the cheek, his beard tickling her lips, then whispered low so only he could hear. "No way I'm throwing you back."

## 26

Julie stared up the pressure ridge at Gunnar helping Mason as he made his way down. The ice popped beneath her, then groaned. The call of the ocean shifting its frozen surface hardly registered anymore. They'd woken to what sounded like a freight train chugging past only to find the small pressure ridge they'd camped near had grown into a jagged beast of a mountain over night with the shifting of the ice.

Jogging in place to warm up, she gritted her teeth as Mason passed a tricky section. The morning sun warmed the ice, making it slicker than snot. At this rate, with the temps warming and the ice thinning, they might never make it to the North Pole.

They had underestimated the time they'd need to get to their destination. While Mason had fantasized about making the same pace as most mushers made running the Iditarod, he'd been realistic in understanding they'd never average seventy miles a day. Even their guess of forty-five miles a day had been off.

Their plan for twenty-eight days on the ice had shifted drastically when they averaged only thirty-five miles a day. Thank God for Saylor and her ability to command. She'd reorganized all the supplies packed for the checkpoints, adding enough food and fuel for the dogs and people to go for forty-five days. They'd been able to clock a faster speed than that, but having the extra supplies helped ease some of the worry.

The only downside? The added weight made navigating the pressure ridges even more treacherous. With no more checkpoints scheduled, they couldn't jettison the supplies that could mean life or death.

A week, maybe a week and a half, longer and they'd be at the Pole. If they didn't hit any snags. She turned her back to the men and scanned the horizon. Clark and Sunny had gone ahead two hours ago to scout a trail. They should be back, but Julie couldn't see a thing but white. The sun reflected off the snow, turning everything into a blank canvas. She'd be glad to see the dark green of the spruce and the deep blue and purples of the mountains when she got back to Alaska.

A shout spun her around just as Mason slid and fell the short distance to the bottom of the ridge. The dogs, finally on flat ground, bolted. Mason's shout at them morphed into a scream of agony. He clutched his leg, the dogs forgotten.

Julie looked from Mason to the disappearing dogs and back. Should she stay and help Mason? If his injury was life-threatening, Gunnar might need her help. If it wasn't, the dogs could be lost forever.

She glanced back at the dogs disappearing into the horizon. They were so far from anything, the dogs would never survive on their own. She couldn't allow that to happen. Plus, they'd need those supplies if they were going all the way to the Pole.

Dashing to her own sled where her team was jumping at the leads to join the race, she yanked the snowhook from the ice. "Hup! Hup!"

She ran between the runners as the dogs picked up speed, only placing her feet on the flat surface when she couldn't keep up with the dogs anymore. Tolstoy followed Mason's sled's trail, his tongue hanging out the side of his mouth. How she was ever blessed with such an amazing lead dog, she'd never know. He could pick a trail through the worst terrain but still listened to commands better than any dog she or her father had ever had.

Squinting against the glare of the sun, she scanned the horizon. Out of all the teams, Mason's was the most unpredictable. They definitely had spunk, but their inability to follow directions had led to more than one incident. Nothing like this, though. Mainly, they liked to pick fights. This latest misadventure may just get them killed.

When she didn't see any sign of them, she huffed out in exasperation. A wind buffeted against her and blew the tracks clear. She glanced behind her only to find her trail filling in faster than a dry riverbed at break-up. If she didn't turn back soon, she might never find her way back.

Tolstoy howled, whipping Julie's head around. He turned the team left around the base of a jumble of ice, and Julie leaned into the sharp curve. Just ahead, Mason's team trotted along a lead of open water like they were taking a stroll in the park. If she didn't approach them right, they'd take off again, thinking they were racing.

The ice stacked up on the left of her with the open lead to the right. Up ahead, the ice ended at the open water in a natural blockade. If she could just get her team close enough, she'd be able to block the renegades in.

"Come on, Stoy, let's box them in." Her encouragement did what she'd hoped.

The sled nearly flew across the ice. Her dogs yipped in excitement, their mouths smiling with their tongues hanging out. There was no way she could give this up. They loved the race too much.

Heck, she loved it.

She sent up a prayer that she hadn't miscalculated and that no dogs would get injured and urged her team faster. They eased up on the left of Mason's team. His dogs veered right, causing the sled to skid along the edge of the ice, tipping precariously over the edge.

"Whoa."

*Please let them listen.*

She almost cheered when their pace slowed a bit. She swallowed the sound down when the ice broke beneath the empty sled. It careened toward the sea, dragging the wheel dogs with it. If they went in, they'd either drown or die from hypothermia.

"Ha. Ha!" Julie had never yelled the command for turning left as loud as she did.

Tolstoy veered, turning to run along the fast approaching ice barrier.

"Good boy, Stoy!" She willed Mason's lead to do the same.

He lived up to his name, Loki, choosing to continue forward. Obstinate dog.

"Loki!" She put all the authority she had in her voice

as Mason's wheel dogs let out frantic barks as the sled dragged them over the edge. "Ha. Ha, Loki."

The difficult dog finally listened and veered left.

"Good boy. Now, get up! Hup!"

Loki yipped, and the team lunged against their leads that pulled them backward. The wheel dogs' heads peeked from the edge, their paws clinging to the ice.

"Good dogs. Keep it up."

Julie didn't want her team to stop, afraid that Loki would as well, but she had to get control of the empty sled. She jumped from her sled and dashed to Mason's, still hanging over the edge. Just as she reached the front of it, the ice broke beneath it. Her heart flew into her throat as she tipped toward the open ocean.

## 27

Gunnar raced to Mason with the first-aid supplies, scanning the horizon for a sign of Julie. The wind picked up and blew snow around, obscuring the area. He didn't like that she'd gone after the dogs alone, but he also understood that she'd had to. If she didn't catch those dogs, they'd die. She couldn't just let that happen.

Still didn't make the wait for her to return any easier.

If Clark and Sunny would just show back up, Gunnar could take off after Julie and help her. He knew better than most that when things went sideways, one had to do whatever they could to turn it back on the skids. Julie's action took her after the dogs. He had to focus on Mason.

Gunnar snapped the flap open on the tent he'd hastily put up and climbed inside. Mason leaned against a set of packs propped up behind him, his face contorted in pain. How Mason had fallen worried Gunnar. They might have bigger issues than runaway dogs.

"All right. Let's see what we've got." Gunnar worked off Mason's layers to examine the injury.

Hopefully, it was just a sprain, but even that could derail their expedition.

"I think it's broken." Mason hissed, then cursed low as Gunnar worked the thick clothing off.

Gunnar grunted his response. No use wasting words of comfort, if that was the case. While the expedition was partly a marketing ploy for Nordic Nibbles, Mason mostly wanted to conquer the impossible. It was his way of encouraging others to not let their limitations stop them. Gunnar admired Mason's drive, but how he weaved philanthropy into the adventures was why Gunnar agreed to come.

When Gunnar pulled the last layer of clothing off and exposed the bulge under the skin on the shin, Mason groaned and whacked his head against the packs.

"Looks like you were right." Gunnar bent over the leg to examine it more closely, then dug through the first-aid kit for morphine and ice packs.

Dogs barking and the slide of runners against snow filled the air. A minute later, the tent flap whipped aside, and Clark crawled in. He took one look at Mason, his forehead creasing in concern.

"What happened?" He crawled the rest of the way in and ripped off his mittens with his teeth.

"I took the fast way off the ridge." Mason gritted his teeth.

"Don't you know that never works out like you hope?" Sunny scooted around Gunnar and kneeled next to Mason's head.

"You'd think I'd know that by now." He leaned his head back and closed his eyes.

"Think you can handle this?" Gunnar injected Mason's leg with morphine as he talked to Clark. "I need to go help Julie."

"Where is she?" Sunny asked, pushing Gunnar toward the door.

"Mason's dogs took off."

Gunnar stared at Clark, waiting for an answer. Gunnar knew the man had the expertise to handle any medical emergency, but Gunnar couldn't leave without knowing.

"We've got this." Clark waved Gunnar off. "Nothing we haven't seen before."

Gunnar barreled out of the tent and ran to his dog team, kicking them to action with a sharp command. He needed to find Julie's trail before the weather covered it. If the wind got any worse, she'd be stuck in a white out alone. All kinds of dangers threatened in this barren landscape. It was why they never went off on their own. They all had emergency beacons on, but if the wind picked up and Julie wasn't able to set up the tent by herself, she'd freeze before help could come. Heck, she could mush through it, trying to get back, and run straight into a lead of water and drown.

That image broke Gunnar into a cold sweat, and he urged the dogs to run faster. Julie could handle anything the wilderness threw at her on her own. He knew that, but he didn't want her to have to. Not anymore.

Snow pelted his burning cheeks like little razors. He dug in his pocket for his goggles. The runner hit a bulge in the snow, and Gunnar lost his balance. He gripped the handle, the snow and ice rushing too close to his face as his feet dragged behind him.

With a roar, he pulled on the handlebars to hike himself up, the muscles in his shoulders and arms burning. His feet skipped along the surface. He placed them on the runners, but they landed on the ends and slid right off. Pulling himself farther up, his feet finally found purchase on the rough grips on the footboards.

He leaned over the handlebars, huffing to catch his breath. The skin on his face burned even more. If he didn't get his goggles on, he'd end up with frostbite.

Standing straight, he flinched at the sight of Julie mushing toward him.

"Whoa, pups." Gunnar pressed on the claw brake and lifted his arm in a wave.

Julie copied the motion, slowing her approach. She'd hooked the two dog teams up one after the other in a long train of fur. Mason's sled attached to the dogs, followed by Julie's. Loki and his cohorts ran with perfect manners for once. Gunnar dug out his goggles and slid them on as she stopped her sled beside him.

"Having troubles?" The laughter in her voice pushed all the worry and fear away.

"Saw that, huh?" Gunnar looked behind him, then adjusted his coat.

"I thought for sure I was about to chase down another runaway team."

She pulled her goggles and face covering off, her smile so wide and beautiful Gunnar wanted to close the distance between them and kiss her until they both were out of breath. Making out in the freezing cold was a stupid thought. Not only would there be the potential for snot—the Arctic made one's nose run like a faucet—but their mouths would probably freeze together. He took a deep breath and tightened his hold on the handlebar.

"You okay, then?" He had to ask, make sure she wasn't hurt.

"Yeah. Just dangled over open water for a bit before Loki decided to stop being a lug and pull."

Julie shrugged like almost drowning in ice cold water wasn't a big deal, but her words hit Gunnar in the chest like a sledgehammer. He'd almost lost her—again.

He slammed his snowhook into the ground, pushed his goggles up, and stalked the four feet separating them. Her eyes widened, but she didn't draw back. Stopping so the toes of their boots touched, he pulled one mitten off and gently touched the back of his fingers to her chapped cheek.

"I'm glad you're safe." He trailed his fingers along her jaw and down her neck.

She grabbed the front of his coat and closed the distance. Her soft kiss burst the embers to a flame that had never extinguished, though he had buried them deep. Her cold lips were rough against his own cracked ones. His fingers warmed as he slid his hand into her hood to cup her head. He rubbed the length of her neck with his thumb, and she shivered.

They really shouldn't be kissing. Mason would need an evac, and their expedition had failed. Gunnar would have plenty of time to kiss her now that they would head back to Alaska. He would make sure of that. But, with her arm anchored around his back and a soft moan rising from her throat, a polar bear would have to come and drag him away to get him to stop.

## 28

It was a good thing Julie's goggles had the added fabric on the bottom that covered the rest of her face. She hadn't stopped smiling like a loon the entire way back to camp and the thirty minutes it took her and Gunnar to get the dogs settled. Clark and Sunny had already set up the second tent and had snow melting for the dogs.

Stomping to the tent Mason lay injured in sobered Julie's soaring mood. She hated that he'd been hurt, hated that they'd have to call the expedition when they were so close. The night before, Gunnar had pulled up their location on the GPS and informed them they were only a week away, shorter if they could keep the decent pace they'd settled into the last week.

But with one wrong step, the expedition had failed.

She scanned the dogs curled into their straw beds and the sleds stocked with supplies. Her gaze traveled farther out to the horizon and the variations of blue showing salty ice newly formed from the constant shifting of the ocean. Soon, the sun would set low in the south, and the ice and snow would turn brilliant shades of pink and orange like a final bow before the curtain closed.

Sure, there'd been times she doubted why she'd come. The frigid temperatures, brutal winds, and loneliness that came from hours of mushing often made her introspection turn negative, especially at first. Each day she pushed farther, and each night that filled with camaraderie edged the pessimistic self-talk further into the back of her mind.

She was a part of the team because she'd earned the spot. Not because of her father's reputation. Nor because of their kennel's. Her dedication to the sport of mushing and days and years spent in the rugged Alaskan wilderness earned her this once in a lifetime experience.

Even though they wouldn't make it to the Pole, she would forever remember the adventure for how it showed that her passion for mushing was her own. Born from legacy. Frozen into her soul through miles of hardship.

"I'm gonna miss this." She blinked the moisture away as footsteps crunched behind her.

Gunnar stopped beside her, wrapping one hand around her back and pulling her into a side hug. "Me too."

She leaned into his side, a ghost of the gleeful grin returning. Even if they didn't reach the finish line, she still received a prize worth more than gold. Having Gunnar back in her life beat mushing to the North Pole, paws down.

"Let's go see when the plane will be here." She pulled

him toward the tent, smiling when he unzipped it and motioned her in like the gentleman he was.

The tent seemed to shrink as the four mobile members of the team squeezed around an outstretched Mason. Pain pulled his mouth tight, and Julie patted his shoulder gently in comfort. If she could give him a hug, she'd give him a big one. The poor guy had planned this trip for five years. The last two, it took up most of his focus. Miserable couldn't begin to explain how he must feel.

Julie sniffed. "Tough break." She slapped her hand over her mouth. "I didn't mean it like that."

Her eyebrows went to her hairline as she darted her gaze to everyone. How could she be so insensitive? She didn't need the propane stove burning in the corner to heat her cheeks. Her humiliation did a fine job.

Mason chuckled, then guffawed. His shoulders shook as the loud sound filled the tent. Everyone joined in the laughter, and the tension eased through the thin tent fabric.

"When does the evac arrive?" Gunnar rubbed his hand across her shoulder and got right to business.

"There's a storm south of here, so it won't be able to come until the weather clears." Sunny sighed, pouring hot water into a mug lined up next to three others, and chocolate-scented steam wafted into the air.

"Okay, do we have enough medical supplies to keep gimpy comfortable? There's no worry of infection setting in or him losing circulation to his foot?" Gunnar shot the questions at Clark.

"From what I can tell, it's a clean break and shouldn't

cause issues, other than the obvious." Clark checked Mason's leg and adjusted the ice pack.

"So, we wait. There are plenty of supplies, and as long as the ice doesn't shift much, the open area Mason's dogs took off down makes a perfect runway." Gunnar shifted to his knees, and Julie pressed her lips to keep a chuckle in, amused at his military tone. "I'm going to organize our supplies. Get us set up for long-term."

"Nope." Mason sighed. "You're going to get supplies moved to yours and Julie's sleds." His determined stare shifted from Gunnar to her. "You two are finishing."

"What? No." Julie shook her head.

"Yes." Mason grimaced as he pushed himself to sit up. "Julie, we've worked too hard and too long to give up now, especially when we are so close."

"But, I—"

"We're a team. If you two make it, then it's a win for all of us." Mason talked over her.

"But what if the rescue plane can't make it? What if your injury turns septic or something?" Her eyes bounced between all of them. "Shouldn't Gunnar be here to help Clark? I mean ... his medical experience is the reason he's on the team."

Why was she arguing? She wanted to finish and make it to the Pole. It just didn't feel right leaving the others behind.

"The storm is only supposed to last a day or two." Clark took the mug Julie handed to him. "It'll be fine. With Sunny's experience guiding up Mount Denali, she has more than enough skills to help."

Julie pushed her fingers along her eyebrows, her head shaking in disbelief. Pairs went to the North Pole every year. Heck, people ventured solo on cross-country skis. It'd be fine with the two of them going on, but was it right?

"Julie, it's why we had a big team to begin with, remember? Best back-up plan, just like Peary's expedition that reached the Pole first all those years ago." Mason patted her on the leg.

"His claim was debunked. He stopped sixty miles too short." She rested her hands in her lap.

"All the more reason for you two to keep going." Mason grabbed her hand and gave it an encouraging squeeze.

"What do you say, Jules?" Gunnar shifted next to her, a thread of excitement she remembered well from high school laced in his voice. "Want to go on an adventure with me?"

"Always." Her answer sprang from her lips the instant his question finished.

His toothy smile split his bearded face and sent dragonflies hovering in her stomach. She hadn't gotten this excited since their trips in high school. They'd always taken care of each other then, getting to their goals with no life-threatening incidents. They could make the next two-hundred thirty miles together safely.

She bit her bottom lip and tried to focus on what Mason jabbered on about, but only one thought raced through her head. She and Gunnar were about to be very, very alone. No one would be around to interrupt their kissing. She unzipped her coat, suddenly roasting in her layers.

## 29

Two days later, Gunnar quadruple-checked the dogs' lines and the stakes keeping them put. He'd thought he'd been diligent before, but now that it was just him and Julie, his meticulous need for precision had turned obsessive. Julie's safety, her life, depended on him being vigilant and thorough in every aspect of their day. It exhausted him, but he'd take the stress any day if it meant he could be with Julie. He wouldn't let her down—not again.

He scanned the horizon one last time while he yanked on the line he'd run from the tent to the dogs in case a blizzard blew in. The cold spiked through his thin gloves he wore when he needed nimble fingers, causing him to shiver. Everything was as settled as it could be outside. Time to get warm.

His mouth twitched on one side. He and Julie had been so fatigued the night before after battling a head-wind all day, they'd barely let the freeze-dried dinner plump up before they inhaled it and rolled into bed. Maybe tonight he could sneak in some snogging, as her father used to say.

Gunnar smiled at the memory of him and Julie jumping apart every time Mr. Sparks hollered that up the stairs. That man had always seemed to know when kissing happened.

He wasn't there to stop any making out now.

No one was.

The twitch of Gunnar's mouth turned into a full-blown smile as anticipation surged like salmon racing upriver. He unzipped the tent flap, then took a deep breath to calm his racing heart. No use startling Jules with a giddy expression plastered on his face.

Ducking into the tent, he caught the slump of her shoulders and the way the corners of her mouth pulled down like all her energy had drained from her. While the soft smile she sent his way as he pulled off his boots brightened her face, it didn't hide her weariness. Was it wrong to drag her the rest of the way to the Pole?

What if her body wasn't strong enough for the rigors the brutal trail required of her? They'd never talked about her cancer after that night at the pool. What if in his eagerness to have this adventure with her like they used to, he put too much of a demand on her? The happy salmon in his gut turned to hungry orca, ripping at him from inside. What if he couldn't keep her safe?

"Just another minute and dinner will be done." Julie pointed to a mug steaming next to the stove. "I made you tea."

"Thanks."

Gunnar pulled off his parka and hung it on the hook attached to the side of the tent by the little propane stove. Any moisture collected in it hopefully would evaporate before they tucked in for the night. Next, he stripped off his snow pants, hoping the mechanical movements of getting settled for the evening would calm his racing thoughts and ease the gnawing pain in his gut.

He'd been trained to keep his cool, wore the distinction of pararescueman perfectly. Put him around Julie, and his control faltered. Too many emotions and worries battled against his mastered vigilance. The problem was, he didn't just want her safe. He wanted her healthy … happy. Making sure that happened went beyond the mechanical efficiency drilled into him by years of war.

"I'm so tired of mushing in the inside of a ping-pong ball, I'd welcome some pressure ridges or leads of water to break the monotony up." Julie sighed and stirred the pouch of food before extending it to him.

"Yeah. The cloud cover and wide expanse certainly make everything flat white." Gunnar hadn't ever experienced such sameness before in all his travels. "Though I think I'll stick with the dome of snow as opposed to the treacherous ridges."

Especially after what happened with Mason.

"We've made good speed the last two days. We keep this up, and we'll be to the Pole lickety-split." She took a bite of chowder.

He grinned at her expression. The more she talked, the more the tension eased from her body. He loved that being with him did that to her. Shoot, talking with anyone would probably relieve the stress. Mushing was such a solitary endeavor and running through the vast sameness as they had for the last two days magnified the loneliness of the sport.

"Just as long as we're safe, I don't care how fast we get there." Gunnar sighed around his last bite and watched Julie's mouth lift before she took a drink.

What he wouldn't give to pull her close right now and kiss a trail from the corner of her mouth to that sensitive spot she used to have behind her ear. Was it still there? Would she still purr that mewing sound she always made? Gunnar snatched the mug of tea up and chugged a drink, scalding the back of his throat.

"We only have two donuts left." Julie put her trash away and brushed her hands together. "Do we save them for another night or plow through them now?"

"I have a better idea." He blew on the tea, peeking at her over the rim. "I brought you something."

"What?"

Her mouth flew open, and her cheeks flushed a pretty pink. She covered her smile with the tips of her fingers. That wouldn't do. He grabbed her hand and rubbed her palm before bringing her fingers to his lips and kissing them. Reluctantly, he let them go and pointed to his pack.

"In the front pocket." He hid his anticipation for her reaction by taking a drink.

"You remembered." She pulled out the Reese's Pieces and turned the bag over in her hands.

"I remember everything." Setting the mug aside, he pushed her hair over her shoulder.

She tilted her head to the side, her muscles relaxing beneath his touch. Just as he leaned in to test if that spot behind her ear was still sensitive, she straightened and her brow creased. Her hand slowly reached into his pack and pulled out her two letters.

"I can't believe you still have these." Her soft words, while not harsh or pained, cut deep into his heart.

He'd been such a fool, a coward. He removed his hand from her shoulder and picked his tea back up. Guilt turned the tea bitter.

"I'm glad they brought you comfort." She ran her finger over his name on the envelope. "Glad you didn't open them."

"Chump move on my part."

"No." She set the candy and letters down. "Your job needed your focus. I knew that. I wouldn't change what happened for anything."

He snorted a humorless laugh and slammed his empty mug onto the crate. "You needed me."

"I wanted you, but I didn't need you." Julie took his hand in hers. "I needed to learn that I had strength on my own. That I didn't need you rescuing me all the time. If you had been there to help, I never would've found that out."

He got that. He did. Though her strength had always impressed him, drawing him to her. Maybe he had been the one that had needed her rescuing him all along.

Made sense.

He'd certainly clung to her letters like they were the only lifeline to reality—to peace—when his world was overrun with brutal conflict. Where she'd pushed past her leaning on him, he'd clutched her memory close. Replayed their life together so many times, all other memories of his childhood faded to dull gray.

Between the two of them, Julie possessed all the strength.

Bravery too.

He'd siphoned all he could from her, bulking up his own gutlessness. Shutting down all emotion so he could do his job, then coming back to her swooping handwriting across the envelope and charging up with her compassionate strength like some robot.

"I don't regret what happened." Julie tucked the letters back in their spot and snatched the candy back up. "Well, that's not entirely true. I regret one thing."

She rolled the bag in her hand, staring at it, but her eyes were unseeing. He'd disappointed her in so many ways. How could she only have one regret? His numbered so many he could walk from the North Pole to the South and back and not step on one twice.

"I ... I wish the cancer had waited a few more months. That the cancer had spared our son." She swallowed, a tear tracing down her cheek.

"We had a son?" Gunnar brushed the pad of his thumb across her skin and dried the tear. His heart clenched at the news, renewed pain spiking him with the loss.

"Yeah." She closed her eyes and leaned into his touch. "Losing him was worse than all the rest combined—the cancer, the treatment—all of it."

"I can't imagine what you went through."

She turned and kissed his palm. The quick pressure exploded heat in his hand that spread up his arm like he held a flare on the hot end. Focusing back on the candy, she shook the bag and cringed.

"You should've seen me. I lost all my hair." She

smiled, shaking her head in lightheartedness. "When it started growing back in, Saylor would put it in these ridiculous little ponytails all over my head. We'd spike them up, then rub different colors of hair chalk on each spike. I'd go like that to the treatment center and joke with the other patients about what they had to look forward to."

Just like Jules to lift others up even though she had to have been suffering herself.

"I bet you looked beautiful. Gorgeous, just like always." Gunnar meant every word.

She was so breathtaking, it hurt to be near her. He ran his fingers through the ends of her hair, wishing he'd been the one helping her laugh through the treatments.

"I lost other things too."

The joviality in her tone faltered. She placed the candy down and looked at him. His muscles froze, like he was bracing for the impact of an incoming explosion.

"They had to take everything, my uterus and tubes. All of it had to go." Her voice cracked, sending shards of shrapnel into his chest.

She'd always gone on and on about wanting a big family like his. Said being an only child was too lonely. Of course, all her talk of children and dreams had stopped shortly after he'd started spouting his stupid plan of cutting ties when he joined the military. Her dreams, though, thoughts of a handful of children or more with her caring spirit and his sense of adventure, had set up a tent in his brain like some vendor at the county fair. Each time he ventured a peek, he wanted to buy the entire inventory.

"I'm sorry, honey."

She sniffed with a shrug. "Made it easy to focus on mushing and helping Dad build the kennel into something amazing. Who'd want someone with so much baggage and no chance of having a family?"

"I would." The words burst from his mouth, throwing all his hopes into the still, chilled air.

Her head jerked up, her eyes wide on her face. He ran his hand down her side and planted it behind her so he leaned into her. Crowding in so her shoulder pressed against his chest, he inhaled the cocoa lingering on her breath.

"I do ... want you. Always." He pressed his forehead to hers. "My heart is yours. Always has been. Always will be until the day I die and through to eternity."

Her breath shuddered as she dropped the candy into her lap, wrapped her fingers in his shirt, and pressed her lips to his. His pulse fired like a 50 cal in his ear as napalm blasted through his veins. Their lips moved in frantic, desperate movements. Joy flooded his brain, sending every one of his cells into a buzzing frenzy. He hadn't lived the years without her. No, he'd simply survived, trudging through the drought his leaving her had made of him.

This ... she was life.

She pulled him closer, one fist still gripping his shirt, while the other speared through his hair. Every follicle stood on edge like they were all reaching for her touch. The skin on his scalp tingled every place her fingers explored.

Wrapping his hand around her hip, he pulled her onto his lap. He needed her closer. He trailed his lips along her jaw to the spot he loved below her ear. The strangled sound in her throat and her palm sliding over his chest and around his side to pull him closer had him smiling against her neck.

The hug of her legs tightened around him. She was his. He'd never let her go now.

## 30

Julie eased over the pressure ridge as a bead of sweat raced down her spine, chilling her already clammy skin. Her calls of encouragement to her dogs bolstered her bravery as much as theirs. Not that they needed it.

She definitely did.

Why had she complained about the boringness of the other days the night before? She'd jinxed them if she believed in such a thing. She'd gladly mush through a ping-pong ball of white any day over this mess.

While the ridge wasn't as high as most they'd traversed, its constant shifting and groaning beneath her feet unnerved her like a monster waiting to eat her alive. Gunnar glanced back at her from where he guided her lead dog, Tolstoy, through the jumbled ice.

"Okay?" The concern in his eyes warmed her chilled body.

"Yeah." She was more than okay.

After their talk and kissing last night, she could probably fly the rest of the way to the Pole. Her cheeks warmed at the memories of his touch. The way he'd whispered her name as he kissed down her neck and along her collarbone—oh man, if she didn't stop thinking about it, she'd melt the ice beneath her.

The ground shifted under her feet like her thoughts really had compromised its already sketchy structure. The hair on the back of her neck rose, and she shivered.

She wanted off this ridge.

Now.

"Good dogs. Let's g—" Her words cut off as the ice collapsed from under her.

Her scream mixed with the dogs' yips as the sled fell into a crevice. The runners slammed against the ice wall, her hands slipping from the handlebar with the jolt. She adjusted her grip, her hanging body swaying with the sled.

"Julie!" Gunnar's yell focused her.

"I'm here." She hollered back, squeaking when her fingers slipped.

If she didn't get a better grip on the sled, she'd fall. She glanced over her shoulder, her eyes widening and head swimming at the sight. The bottom of the crevice yawned dark, with giant ice spears for teeth jutting up from a black ocean.

She'd never survive a drop there.

The sled lurched farther down, loosening her hold even more. *Move, Jules.* She flexed her arms, tightened her core, and pulled inch by inch until she could get her armpit nestled on the handlebar.

"Jules?" Gunnar called over the ledge, but she couldn't catch her breath.

She sucked in the frozen air, causing her to cough.

"Jules, honey, talk to me."

His calm, steady voice eased her fear. He'd help her out of this. She just had to stay strong and focused.

"I'm fine." She took another shaky breath. "Just taking a break. You know, enjoying the scenery."

"Well, why don't you get up here so we can enjoy it together?"

She glanced up, needing to see him, but the supplies on the sled blocked her view. "Use those PJ muscles and pull me up, and I'll watch clouds form all day with you."

The sled jiggled, making her stomach swoop. She slammed her eyes closed and tucked her head against her arms.

"You need to climb up." Gunnar's words shattered what composure she had left, leaving her shaking from head to toe. "The edge is too slick. There's nowhere for me to get footing."

She swallowed and peered down into the monster's mouth. Could she let go of what little stability she had? She'd be climbing with nothing to catch her if she lost her hold.

"Honey? You need to go ... now." The strain in Gunnar's voice made his words hard to hear.

There was no way he'd let go if the sled slipped. He would go down with her. All her dogs too. They'd all drown in the freezing ocean, more than likely buried under the shifting ice. No one would know what happened.

Her terror turned to determination. She wouldn't let her fear kill them all. Not when she had just gotten Gunnar back. She planned on living a long life with him, not dying like that depressing movie about the Titanic.

"I'm coming. Hold tight."

She ripped her mittens off with her teeth and shoved them into her parka pockets. Without them, her fingers would get cold fast, but with them, she couldn't get a firm grasp. She searched the sled for the best handholds, mapping her way as best she could up the supplies.

At the last minute, she unsnapped the lock on her wrist sheath for her small knife. If the sled started going, she'd cut the thing loose and save Gunnar and her dogs.

"Moving," she hollered, pulling herself higher onto the handlebars.

She kicked one leg until the toe landed on the edge of the cargo basket, then pressed with all her might to get herself further over the bar. Wrapping her fingers around a strap holding a crate down, she pulled. The material cut into her already chapped skin, making her fingers bleed.

She inhaled sharply, ignoring the pain as best she could, and reached for the next strap. She needed to hustle, but moving fast meant less caution. Did caution matter when one hung over an ice monster waiting to swallow her whole?

Just a few more handholds and she could use her feet to climb. She growled as her muscles shook with fatigue. Why did she have to choose the extra-long sleds for the expedition?

She could see the ridge now.

Her wheel dogs' feet were planted precariously close to the edge. Their entire bodies shook as they strained against the weight of the sled. Gunnar stood a little farther back, his face tensed with exertion, more than likely positioning himself in front of the wheel dogs' neckline. It's what she'd do to avoid getting tangled with the dogs.

When her feet touched the handlebars, she stood, reaching for the strap closest to the front of the sled. She was almost there. Just a few more feet and she'd be safe.

As she gripped the strap, the hook holding the skinny fabric to the sled came loose. She screamed as her bloodied hand slipped. A crate tumbled out of its spot, knocking her in the head and bouncing off of her back. Stars exploded in front of her eyes.

The swaying of the sled broke the edge of the crevice free. Her wheel dogs yipped in fear as they fell and crashed against the crevice wall. Panic tumbled in her, making her vision blur. Gunnar's eyes bulged as he looked down at her. The veins in his neck throbbed with the strain of holding them.

They would not make it.

She couldn't let them all die.

Clambering as fast as she could, she ignored the frantic barking of her dogs. She reached the brush bow of the sled and steadied herself in the space left by the crate. Her heart beat in her chest like someone was taking a sledgehammer and ramming it against her ribs. She could do this, save them.

She yanked her knife out of its sheath on her forearm and gazed up at Gunnar.

"Jules—" The sled plunging farther down cut off his words as he adjusted his hold.

Grabbing the gangline with one hand, she sliced with the other. When the rope held, she hacked again, trying not to let Gunnar's protests stop her. The knife chopped almost through. The thin threads still holding frayed in slow motion. She held her breath, the sledgehammer of her heart pounded loud in her ears.

She stared up at Gunnar, his eyes bright with unshed tears. The thread snapped, and she gulped down a scream as the sled dropped from her feet. Her slick fingers slid along the rope.

She dropped her knife and reached up with her other hand. The rope was coated in her blood and slipped beneath her skin. Without the weight of the sled, the rest of her dogs yanked her and the wheel dogs upward, but not fast enough. Desperate to keep her grip, the rope's end got closer and closer as she slid down the rope.

## 31

The sudden release of the weight on the rope had Gunnar stumbling backward. His heart flew into his throat, stifling his anguished scream. A splash shattered in his brain, jolting him from his shock. He had to get to Julie. There wasn't life without her.

"Gunnar, I'm slipping." Julie's muffled cry for help penetrated his grief-soaked mind.

"Get up, dogs. Let's go." He forced the command through a throat that didn't want to work, adjusting his grip on the rope and running with the dogs.

He turned at the frantic yips behind him, encouraging the dogs to keep going. Julie's wheel dogs clambered over the edge. Gunnar dashed around them, dropping to his knees at the edge of the crevasse just as Julie's hands slipped from the rope.

He grabbed her coat with one hand and the rope with the other as it raced past him. Roaring as fiery pain tore through his arms, he let the momentum of the dogs running pull Julie over the icy lip. Only when she was completely over the edge and the dogs had dragged them several feet did he let go of the rope, calling for the dogs to stop.

He scrambled to her, a sob ripping from him. "I thought I'd lost you."

"I'm okay." Her weak smile and pale lips tightened his ribs. "I—"

Her eyes rolled into the back of her head as her body went limp. Ripping off his gloves, he cupped her cheeks as he searched for a pulse. When it thumped steady and hard against his fingers, he forced himself to calm down and assess the situation.

He pushed back her hood, sucking a breath through his teeth at the large gash and bump forming just above her temple. Okay. They could deal with that. He couldn't do anything out here exposed to the elements. He needed to get them a shelter.

Yanking her mittens peeking out from her pockets, he gently slid her mangled hands in them to keep them as warm as possible. He then scooped her up into his arms and picked his way off the pressure ridge. Thank God, Julie had trained her dogs so well. They waited at the bottom of the ridge next to his.

He set her down next to his sled and quickly adjusted the supplies so she had a place to ride. When he had her settled and her dogs hooked into his gangline, he hollered for them to go. He'd picked a place to camp while he'd been waiting for her to traverse the ridge. He just needed to get there and make camp faster than he ever had before. A sharp wind hit him in the face, taunting him.

*Please, just let me get her safe.*

An hour and a half later, Gunnar blinked away the sting in his eyes as he bandaged up Julie's hand. The wind and snow pelted the side of the tent like it had the last hour, but he didn't care. He'd almost lost her. Her hands were shredded and swollen. She had a welt on her forehead the size of a boulder and bruises blackened her back.

"I'm fine." Julie sounded dead tired.

Dead. He shuddered at his thought.

"Hey." She touched her fingertips to his cheek, and he closed his eyes. "I'll take a few cuts and a bang on the head. We worked together, figured it out, and made it through."

She trailed her fingers over his beard, making him long to press against her touch. That would only hurt her more. He cupped her hand and softly kissed the tips of her fingers. It was the only part of her hands still exposed after his doctoring.

He gently lifted her other hand to his lips and repeated kissing each tip. What if he couldn't keep her safe? What if the next time they didn't make it through? He couldn't lose her. Would rather be buried alive in an icy tomb than live life without her.

Placing his lips on her wrist, he lingered there, inhaling the smell of snow still clinging to her. She shivered and sighed, her head tipping slightly to the side. He smiled against her soft skin.

What other noises of contentment could he pull from her? He massaged her arm through her sweater, working his way to her shoulder. With each move up, he kissed the area he'd just left. Her eyes drooped closed, and her head fell back, exposing the pale skin of her neck. His gaze zeroed in on her pulse bumping there.

"I've been thinking." Julie's voice was languid and low, like she had to work hard to form words.

He hummed an acknowledgment. He didn't want to think—wanted to push all thoughts bombarding him with fear away. Reaching the top of her shoulder, he nibbled the skin along her collar. Her breath hitched, making his heart race.

"We should still go on, hook the dogs to your sled and make a run for the Pole." She leaned her head as she spoke, giving him better access.

"Jules." He practically growled against her neck, not liking where this conversation was heading. He'd barely gotten his pulse back to normal after her almost death, and she wanted to talk about continuing this Expedition of Doom?

"Think about it."

"No thinking. Not now." He breathed against the spot she loved, thrilled when she let out a low moan.

Her skin felt like velvet against his chapped lips as he made a trail along her jawline to her mouth.

"Gunnar."

His name was more air than solid sound. He'd never tire of hearing her say it. He hovered over her mouth, her shuddering breath against his lips. He shifted and worked his kisses along the opposite jawline.

With a frustrated huff, she pushed against his shoulder with the back of her hand. "At least listen to me."

He nuzzled below her ear and mumbled into her neck. "I'm listening."

"We're only a few days away from the Pole. We have enough food for the dogs and us for five days. All we'd have to do is set up the dog bag, maybe add a sleeping bag inside for extra warmth, and I can ride in the sled." Her words rushed out like she was anxious to get the conversation over with.

"You'll freeze."

"Not necessarily. Not if we do it right."

He did growl this time and pressed his face into her neck. Did he want to risk her getting more injured? She'd be exposed in the sled. Not being able to move and run between the runners when she got cold could let frostbite settle in. Or worse. With her wrapped like a burrito in the bag, if the sled wrecked or fell through another crevice, could she get out?

"Jules."

"Don't answer now." She placed her hands on both sides of his face, forcing him to look at her.

The stark white bandages were just a reminder of how close she'd come to dying.

How he hadn't been able to keep her safe.

How he constantly broke his childhood promise to her to always be there when she needed him.

Constantly picked the coward's way out when it came to her.

"We won't be able to move until this storm passes, anyway." Her gaze bounced left and right like she searched his expression for some hope.

He narrowed his eyes at her. She wanted reassurance that they'd go on, but he couldn't give it. Not with the fear from earlier, the fear of what might wait ahead, still clawing his insides to shreds. If he didn't make the right decision and keep her safe in the mess the expedition had become, how could he ever have the courage to trust himself with her and their future?

## 32

J ulie snuggled up against Gunnar's chest. The heat from his arms wrapped around her and their legs pretzeled together had her warmed all the way to her marrow. The benefits of her sled—with her sleeping bag—plunging into the Arctic Ocean, settled her against a solid chest that rose and fell in a peaceful rhythm. Maybe she should have cut her sled loose miles before.

Two days had passed since they'd set up camp. Forty-eight hours of the wind and snow thrashing against the flimsy, orange fabric of the tent. It had made talking hard. But then again, it'd made snuggling close and kissing that much easier.

She held her breath, twisting her head to hear better. Aside from Gunnar's steady heartbeat thumping in her ear and his entrancing inhales and exhales, she didn't hear a thing. Had the storm finally passed? If so, could she convince Gunnar to make the final push?

She knew the dangers, especially with her bundled

up in a sled bag, unable to move. However, she also knew she didn't want to give up. She'd started this expedition out of anxiousness—desperate to not only honor her father's memory but to keep the kennel going. But along the tough trail, she'd found that mushing was just as much her passion as it had been her father's.

She may have started the journey north because of her family's legacy, but she would finish for herself.

Now, she just needed to convince the reticent warrior holding her tight to come with her.

Leaning a little more away, she stared at his relaxed face. She ran her fingers along his collarbone, following his olive skin to the hair curling against his neck. It'd grown longer in the month they'd been on the trail. He looked a bit wild with his beard and hair grown out.

She loved it, the unrestrained side of him.

Twirling the soft curl through her fingers, she grinned as he pulled her closer with a low hum. Sparks built in her chest like those fireworks her dad used to buy that would snap and sparkle small, only to crescendo to a showering fountain of color. While they hadn't gone beyond kissing, it surprised her the tent hadn't exploded into ten-foot flames from the heat his touch generated in her.

He nuzzled against her neck, his beard tickling her skin. A part of her ignited and thrummed to life, the part she'd worried the cancer had killed. The sensation overwhelmed her, bringing her fully awake from the hibernation she'd been stuck in since her treatments.

Maybe if she would've gotten out more, had actually attempted to date after the cancer, she would have figured that out earlier. Not likely. Not when all the promises for her future, all her love, had been forever tied to Gunnar Rebel.

She couldn't let him distract her now that the storm had passed. Her hands no longer burned from pain. Well, mostly. The swelling on her forehead had subsided and now just sported a nasty bruise, and her back muscles didn't protest every time she moved. She was beat up, sure, but she wasn't immobile.

The last two days, she'd watched the GPS. They'd been continually floating closer to the Pole, like God Himself wanted them to make it. She wouldn't waste that advantage. How would she convince her overprotective boyfriend to go along with it?

Boyfriend?

Is that what he was? It seemed such a juvenile word for how she felt about Gunnar. Maybe not juvenile, more lacking.

Soul mate?

Yes.

Love of her life?

Absolutely.

Yet, they hadn't even talked about what would happen after the expedition finished. Her home was between Glenallen and Valdez while his was in Seward, some seven hours away. Fifteen years she'd helped her father build their facility to a top-notch training center. Could she leave it all for a chance at life with Gunnar?

"Mmm." He kissed behind her ear and along her jaw like he liked, causing her skin to tighten and the comfort of the sleeping bag to get too hot. "Morning, honey."

His hand spread wide against her back as he kissed her softly. The expanse of his palm left her feeling protected, like he'd shield her from any harm. The way he nipped her bottom lip, shooting electricity to her fingers and turning them to sparklers, then gentled his kiss with tender words, left her with a sense of being cherished. Both feelings reenforced his promise he'd made to her all those years ago.

Maybe it hadn't been broken?

Maybe they both had to find themselves in their trials for the promise to be kept?

"I can't believe you're here in my arms." He pushed his hand up her back and into her hair, making every strand ache and tingle. "I've dreamed of holding you like this every time I've closed my eyes since I left."

Even though his kiss was deep and full of restrained desire, he held her loosely, like he gave her the option to leave. She ran her hand around his side, his muscles jumping beneath her touch, and held him flush against her. No matter what, she would not let him go. Whether they pushed on to the Pole—whether she left her home for his—she wasn't letting this man out of her life again.

He buried his face into her neck, his breath hot against her skin. "I keep thinking I'm going to wake up back in my lonely cabin and this would have all been a crazy dream."

"It's not. We're here together." She pushed her fingers through his hair and kissed the top of his head. "I'm here with you ... forever if you want." She took a deep breath, anticipation pressuring up like a shaken soda. "I promise."

The two words were only a whisper, but his fingers froze their soft massage on her back. He pulled back, hope and heat burning in his eyes. His Adam's apple bobbed.

"Another promise?" His voice was low, his body tense with vulnerability. "Even after I broke the last one?"

"No, you never did." She placed her fingertip on his lips when he protested. "You taught me to be strong, to survive. Your lessons when we mushed—thoughts of the hardships and torture you were going through to save others—all of it gave me the courage to fight my own battles. To find my strength to survive." She cupped her still-bandaged palm against his cheek. "No, you kept your promise that you'd always be there for me, just not in the way either of us ever expected. But it was the way both of us needed."

His eyes searched hers, then closed with a shuddering breath. A tear rushed down his cheek, sliding along his beard until it collided with her bandage. She wiped the next one with her thumb and pressed her forehead to his.

"I love you, Julie Karen Sparks." His words hitched, and he took a deep breath. "With everything that is in me."

"Good, because I never stopped loving you." She kissed his lips. "Not one second of the fifteen years"—she kissed him again—"four months"—and again—"and sixteen days since you left for basic."

The last kiss she lingered on the corner of his mouth that always tipped up in amusement. She laughed against his lips as he sat up with a growl, bringing her with him, wrapping her legs around his waist, then pushing her hair behind her ear. His touch was a flame burning heat down her neck.

He tilted his head, his nose rubbing against hers.

When he finally claimed her mouth, his soft and languid kiss shifted to deep and all-consuming. His reverence for her expressed in his trembling fingers as they traced her face, her neck, the curve of her ear, everywhere he could explore, lighting little fires along her skin.

"I can't ... I can't leave you again. Not even for a day," he whispered against her lips, exploding joy through her body.

"Then don't." She leaned back, stared into his eyes, and took a deep breath. She wanted all of it, this man, her dreams, and she was going after it, no matter if others, mainly her cousin, ruffled up like fussy ptarmigans. "Marry me. Stay. Mush the remaining trails of our lives with me."

His smile grew slow and languid like his kiss, turning her to boiling lava. "Now, that sounds like an adventure I can't refuse."

"Good." She tightened her hold on him, kissing him until they were both breathless. "Good, because our first trail is leading us to the North Pole."

He shook his head, but the action held no argument. His gaze traveled over her face as he cupped her neck, his thumbs sliding over her cheekbone and along her jaw. His kiss was quick and soft, full of determination.

"Then, we better stop snogging and get moving." His forced exasperation had her chuckling.

She pecked him one last time and scrambled out of the sleeping bag. They had a lot of work before they could get back on the trail, but she didn't mind. Together, they'd make it all the way to the top of the world. From there, they'd figure out their next adventure.

## 33

Gunnar scanned the white expanse as Julie counted down their approach to the North Pole. He wasn't sure why he expected something other than what they'd experienced the last thirty-one days. Probably Julie's enthusiasm and constant wondering if the Pole would be a jumbled mess, blizzard, or ping-pong ball.

Thankfully, they'd arrived on option four: sunny and calm, with flat snow and ice stretched for miles. For all the obstacles they'd had getting there, he never imagined the last two days would be so easy.

Julie tipped her head back and looked up at him from the sled. She'd taken the face shield off, and a beautiful smile stretched from ear to ear. Because of her, they'd get this experience.

Because of her, his heart had taken residence in his chest again. Somewhere along the last fifteen years, it had packed up, leaving him with a poor mechanical substitute. He'd learned to adjust, to go through the motions of life. But it hadn't been living.

Now, with Julie, life pulsed through him so hard his chest ached.

"We're almost there!" She chugged her hands in the air in a celebratory dancing motion.

This wouldn't do. She couldn't make it to her dream wrapped like a burrito in the sled.

"Whoa," he called to Tolstoy.

Her dog had not been okay with being in the middle of the pack. It was fitting he lead the extra-long team of dogs. Julie had been the one leading them on too.

"Why are we stopping?" Julie twisted on her perch, scanning the area. "We aren't there yet."

He stomped the ice hook into the snow and walked around the sled.

"We're stopping because while it's fitting the queen is perched upon her throne, she deserves to cross the finish line of her own accord." He bowed before unzipping her from the bag.

She shimmied out of her cocoon and stood on the sled. When he reached to help her out, she jumped into his arms, wrapping her legs around his waist, and kissing him hard. Her cold lips felt like frozen jello against his. He'd have to get the tent set up soon to warm her up.

He smiled against her mouth. Just one kiss from her, and he overheated.

"Put me down, you big oaf." She bit his bottom lip, unwrapped her legs, and pushed playfully against his shoulder. "If we don't hurry, the ocean will float us away, and we'll have to walk a mile instead of feet."

"If I remember right, you were the one who jumped

me." He tightened his arm and refused to let go, nuzzling up her jaw to below her ear.

When she tilted her head with a sigh, he opened his arms, dropping her with a smirk. Her shriek and laughter bounced across the snow, through his booted feet, and shot straight to his heart. He rubbed his hand across the fullness there.

"Geesh, stop wasting time. We've got a Pole to conquer." He headed past the dogs, commanding them to stay.

Julie stepped up beside him, the GPS in her hand counting down the longitude degrees to the zero and the latitude to ninety. With the ocean constantly moving the sea ice, there wasn't a way to mark the Pole like the South Pole had. Relying on the GPS unit was the only way they'd know when they made it.

She watched the screen, not paying attention to where she stepped. Not that there was anything to pay attention to. Gunnar dug into his pocket for the special camera Mason had each of them carry to document the expedition. Gunnar had almost forgotten he'd stuck it there so it would have a full charge to record the last steps to the end.

He pressed record and pointed it at Julie. "You ready to stand on the North Pole?"

"Absolutely."

She tore her eyes away from the screen to beam up at him. He leaned down to press his smile to hers. She giggled and bumped his shoulder.

"Stop. You're distracting me." She gave him one last peck, then continued walking.

He zoomed the camera on to the GPS screen, not

wanting a doubt that they made it. When the screen showed ninety degrees latitude and zero longitude, they stopped and slowly spun. There wasn't anything to see but the dogs waiting patiently and white earth with blue sky.

Didn't matter.

Being on the top of the world had Gunnar feeling feet taller. He breathed in the sharp, cold air and stopped turning when he faced Julie.

He'd been wrong.

The most beautiful sight in the world stood right before him. Ice clung to the hair that had escaped from her hat. Her cheeks had pinked in the cold air. Fur from her parka's hood, also jeweled with ice crystals, surrounded her face.

Queen, indeed.

She was the queen of the north.

The queen of his heart.

She tipped her head back and howled. The dogs joined with her, filling the air with the joyous sound. It was just like Julie to include the dogs in the celebration. Dropping his head back and closing his eyes, he let out a long, satisfying howl. When he finished, she gazed up at him, her mittens covering her grin. He pointed the camera at his face and brought his hand up like he spoke into a microphone.

"So, Julie Sparks, now that you've reached the North Pole, what do you plan to do?" He used his best impersonation of a reporter, which came out a weird mix of southern twang and uppity London accent.

She dropped her hands and pulled her bottom lip between her teeth before forcing her expression to somber. "You know what? I think I want to dance." She lifted one eyebrow, her smile turning saucy. "With you."

Warmth radiating through his chest pushed the Arctic cold away. He carefully set the camera up on a chunk of ice, pointing toward Julie, then strode to her to dance on the top of the world. Picking her up, he spun her around so her legs flew out behind her. She half laughed, half cheered as she flung her arms out wide.

He slowed and pulled her as flush to him as two could get with layers and layers of gear on. Swaying to the chorus the dogs still sang, he pushed her hood back. Happiness radiated from her, bouncing off the snow and almost blinding him.

How could life turn around so quickly?

A month and a half before, he'd been resigned to live out his lonely existence in the bleak Alaskan wilderness. Now, the only person who had ever held his heart looked up at him with so much love in her eyes, it made his throat close and his nose sting.

"So now what?" He pushed the words through his dry throat.

"I don't care." She rose onto her tiptoes, her lips brushing his as she whispered, "As long as I'm with you."

"I'm gonna hold you to that promise."

He kissed her, not caring the world would watch on the video still recording. Not caring that the wind picked up and dropped the already frigid temperature even colder. Everything vanished except Julie's soft sigh against his lips and the promise of a life full of love and adventure.

# EPILOGUE

Sunny Rebel looked around her parents' dining room, joy bubbling in her chest like the sparkling water still fizzing in her glass. Her siblings had all made it home for Easter. Even Magnus, who took their last name to a whole new level with his firefighting stunts, had graced them with his presence. The room burst with conversation and laughter. The sound overwhelmed her after a month of the relatively quiet Arctic Ocean, but she basked in it.

Here, with folding tables pushed together and elbows bumping, she didn't have to worry. Here, trust filled her to overflowing. Too bad she couldn't bottle up the excess and take it into the rest of the world.

"So, what are your next plans?" Sadie Wilde, Bjørn's girlfriend, leaned closer to Sunny to be heard.

"I'm going to Dutch Harbor with Astryd and taking a solo sea kayak trip through the islands. Then, later this summer, Tiikâan is going to drop me off in the middle of the 40-mile country, and I'll hike my way out." Sunny took a drink and let the bubbles from her drink soothe her tight throat.

Some of her family hadn't been one hundred percent on board with her solo adventures. Not that they had any say in it. Her being the baby, though she had turned twenty-five over the winter, sometimes made her family overprotective of her.

Who was she kidding?

They were all protective of each other. It was what she loved most about her family, how they all banded together. It was just that their protectiveness had gotten a little heavy handed after her stupidly allowing her business partner to steal all their money and gear and skip town.

She pushed the thought away. That jerk would not ruin her excellent mood. There was no telling when her family would all be together again, and letting her mind stray to the man she'd thought she'd known, the man she'd expected to spend the rest of her life with, wasn't an option.

No one knew the extent of his betrayal. She had kept her massive crush on the downlow. She planned to keep it that way. It was embarrassing enough that everyone knew he'd tricked her out of their business. She wouldn't be adding insult to injury by telling just how far he'd deceived her.

"That should be fun." Sadie smiled at Sunny, her face beaming encouragement. "I've been loving your videos. Keep telling everyone I meet that they have to check them out."

Wow. Sunny loved Bjørn's girlfriend. Not because she liked Sunny's videos, but because of how supportive she was of those around her. She just fit with their family.

Sunny glanced around at Lena's husband, Marshall, and their son Carter. The little guy sat on Dad's lap, chatting wildly in his toddler way that kept them all in stitches and wrapped him around their hearts. Her gaze stopped on Gunnar as he pushed Julie's hair off her shoulder and whispered something in her ear that made her blush.

If those two could find a way to trust each other again after everything they'd been through, could there be hope for Sunny? Maybe. She just didn't know how to get there. Hopefully, it didn't take fifteen years like it had for Gunnar and Julie.

A knock on the door sent Snowflake, her parent's Great Pyrenees, into a riot. Gunnar kissed Julie on the cheek with a chuckle and rushed to the door. Just what did those two have up their sleeve?

"Hello!" Pastor Jerry from their parents' church in Tok ambled in.

"Pastor Jerry, what brings you all the way out here?" Mom stood and pushed on Tiikâan's shoulder. "Son, go grab another chair."

"No need, Katie." Pastor Jerry clapped Gunnar on the shoulder. "Not when we have a wedding to perform."

Sunny didn't think she'd ever heard such silence with her family before. She chuckled as heads turned from Gunnar to Julie and back like a tennis match. Gunnar's smile spreading across his face and the way his eyes shone with an openness and happiness Sunny hadn't seen since he'd left for basic, made her vision blur with stinging tears.

This, this was what trust was—the hope found between these two. Sunny wanted that. Wanted to believe in someone, to know she could depend on them no matter what. She just wasn't sure if she was brave enough to open her heart again.

*Don't miss Sunny's enthralling adventure in Alaska gold country! A Rebel's Trust releases September 6th. Preorder it at a discounted price directly from the author today!*

# ALSO BY SARA BLACKARD

Vestige In Time Series

Vestige of Power

Vestige of Hope

Vestige of Legacy

Vestige of Courage

Stryker Security Force Series

Mission Out of Control

Falling For Zeke

Capturing Sosimo

Celebrating Tina

Crashing Into Jake

Discovering Rafe

Convincing Derrick

Honoring Lena

Alaskan Rebels Series

A Rebel's Heart

A Rebel's Beacon

A Rebel's Promise

A Rebel's Trust

Wild Hearts of Alaska

Wild about Denali

Wild about Violet

### Other Books

Meeting Up with the Consultant

# ABOUT THE AUTHOR

Sara Blackard writes stories that thrill the imagination and strum heartstrings. When she's not crafting wild adventures and sweet romances that curl your toes, she's homeschooling her four adventurous boys and one fearless princess, keeping their off-grid house running (don't ask if it's clean), or enjoying the Alaskan lifestyle she and her Hunky Hubster love. Visit her website at www.sarablackard.com.

74679782R00121